# THE BUMPER OF NEW ZEALAND WILDLIFE



to read
colour
and keep

NH NEW HOLLAND

Dave Gunson

The Maori name for this small parrot is kakariki, which also means 'green'. It likes to eat insects, leaves and fruits.

# Yellow-Crowned Parakeet

**Bumble-bees were brought here from England to help pollinate clover plants. Today, they are found all over the country, living in small colonies in thick undergrowth or below ground. They go from flower to flower, collecting pollen to take back home for food.**

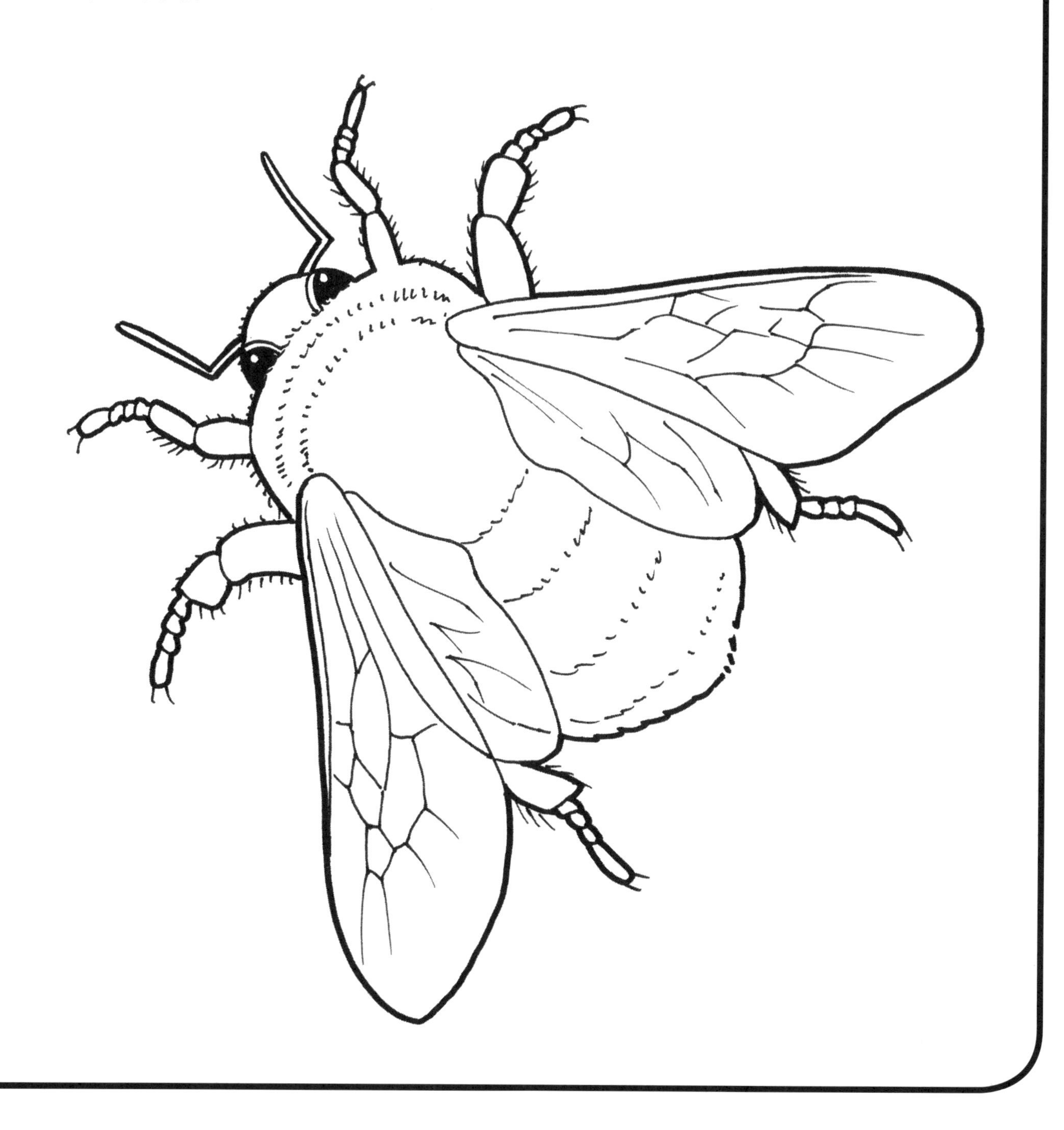

# Bumble-bee

The kingfisher makes its nest in small tunnels that it digs in the side of earth banks. It can often be seen perched on telephone wires as it keeps an eye out for insects or lizards.

## Kingfisher

New Zealand is home to over 40 gecko species. All have a grainy, loose skin. Most gecko species around the world lay eggs, but New Zealand species give birth to live young. It's thought that many can live for up to 30 or 40 years.

# Green Gecko

The kiwi is probably the most famous of all birds in New Zealand. It lives in the forests, and comes out of its burrow at night to dig around in the forest floor with its long bill to find worms and insects. It usually finds food by smell, because its nostrils are at the very tip of its bill!

# Kiwi

**New Zealand's own 'Christmas tree' is common around northern coasts, often growing on steep cliffs and rocks close to the shore. It is a spectacular sight when the scarlet blossoms appear in early and mid summer. A hardy tree, it can live for 500–800 years.**

# Pohutukawa

The sauropod measured about 10 to 14 metres in length. It had lots of small peg-like teeth and ate only plants. Many dinosaurs of this type swallowed stones to help grind up the food in their stomachs.

# Sauropod

**Male and female pairs of coralfish usually bond for life, and make their home in a rocky sea cave or arch, where their striking markings can make them hard to see against the background of the colourful reef. If discovered, a coralfish can lock the spines on its fin upright to stop predators from taking a bite.**

# Lord Howe Coralfish

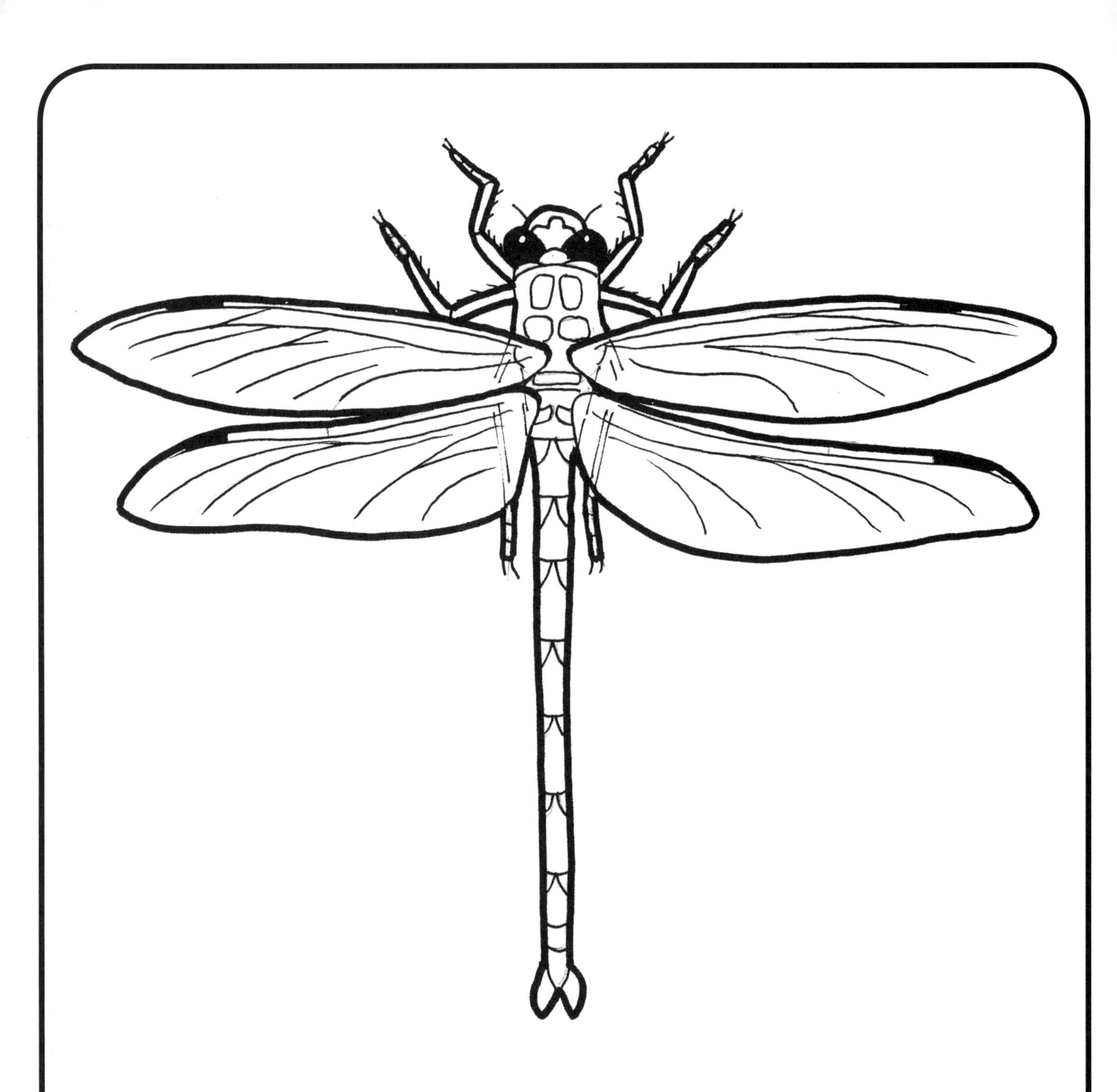

**With wings spanning up to 13 centimetres, this insect can fly powerfully at speeds of up to 60 kilometres per hour. Two pairs of wings allow it to fly like a helicopter: moving up, down, forwards, backwards and sideways, or just hovering as it hunts for small insects to eat.**

# Giant Dragonfly

The nectar-drinking tui is one of our best songbirds: it can sing, whistle, chuckle, cough and even imitate the songs of other birds, as well as copy the sounds of mobile phones and car alarms.

## Tui

**The moa is one of the most famous of all the world's extinct birds. It was one of the largest birds ever to have existed – its shoulder was higher than a man.**

# Moa

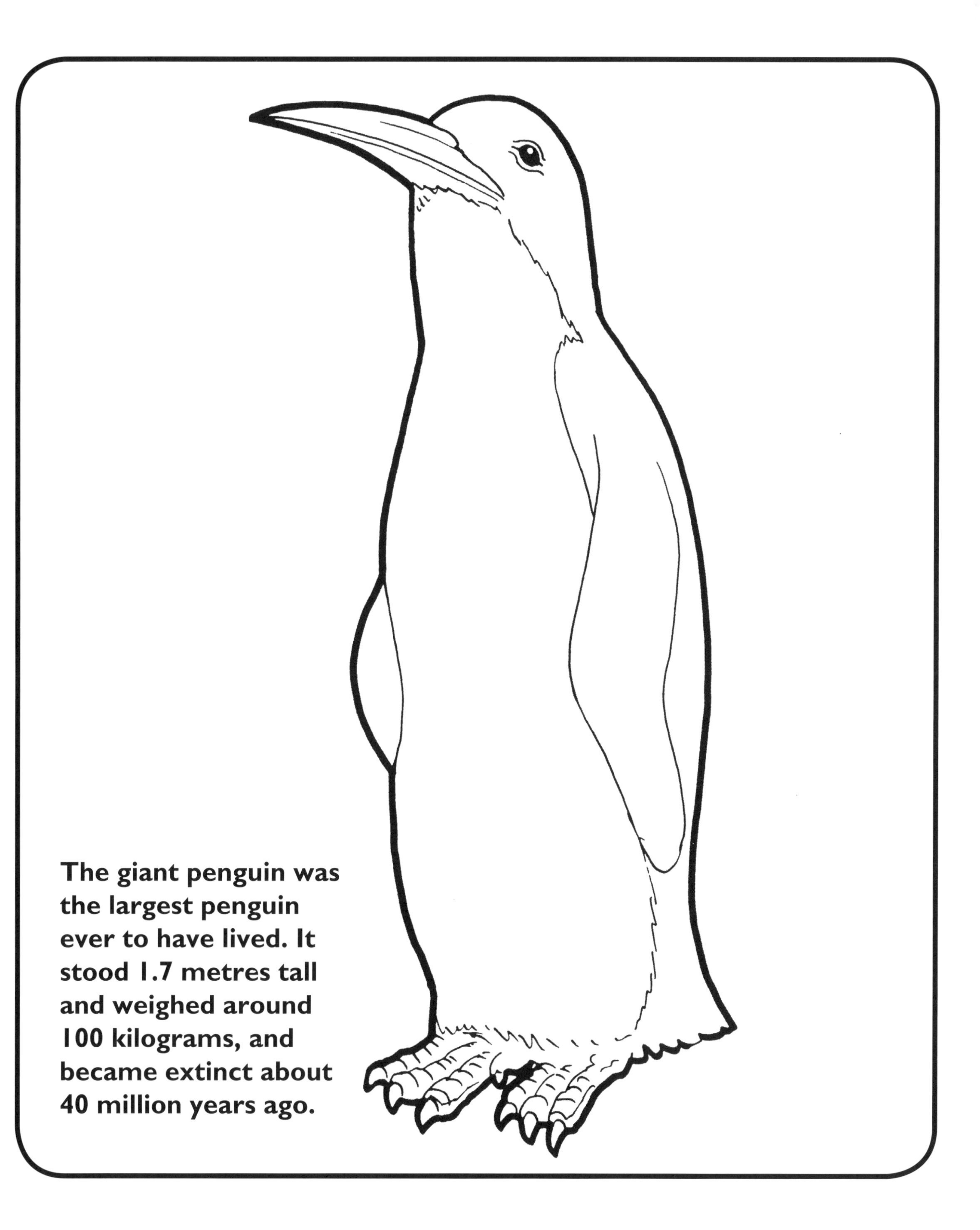

The giant penguin was the largest penguin ever to have lived. It stood 1.7 metres tall and weighed around 100 kilograms, and became extinct about 40 million years ago.

# Extinct Giant Penguin

**Bright green and leaf-shaped, this insect is hard to see as it rests on plants in the garden. The katydid makes a zip-zip call, and its name comes from the call of an American species, which sounds like Katy did – Katy didn't.**

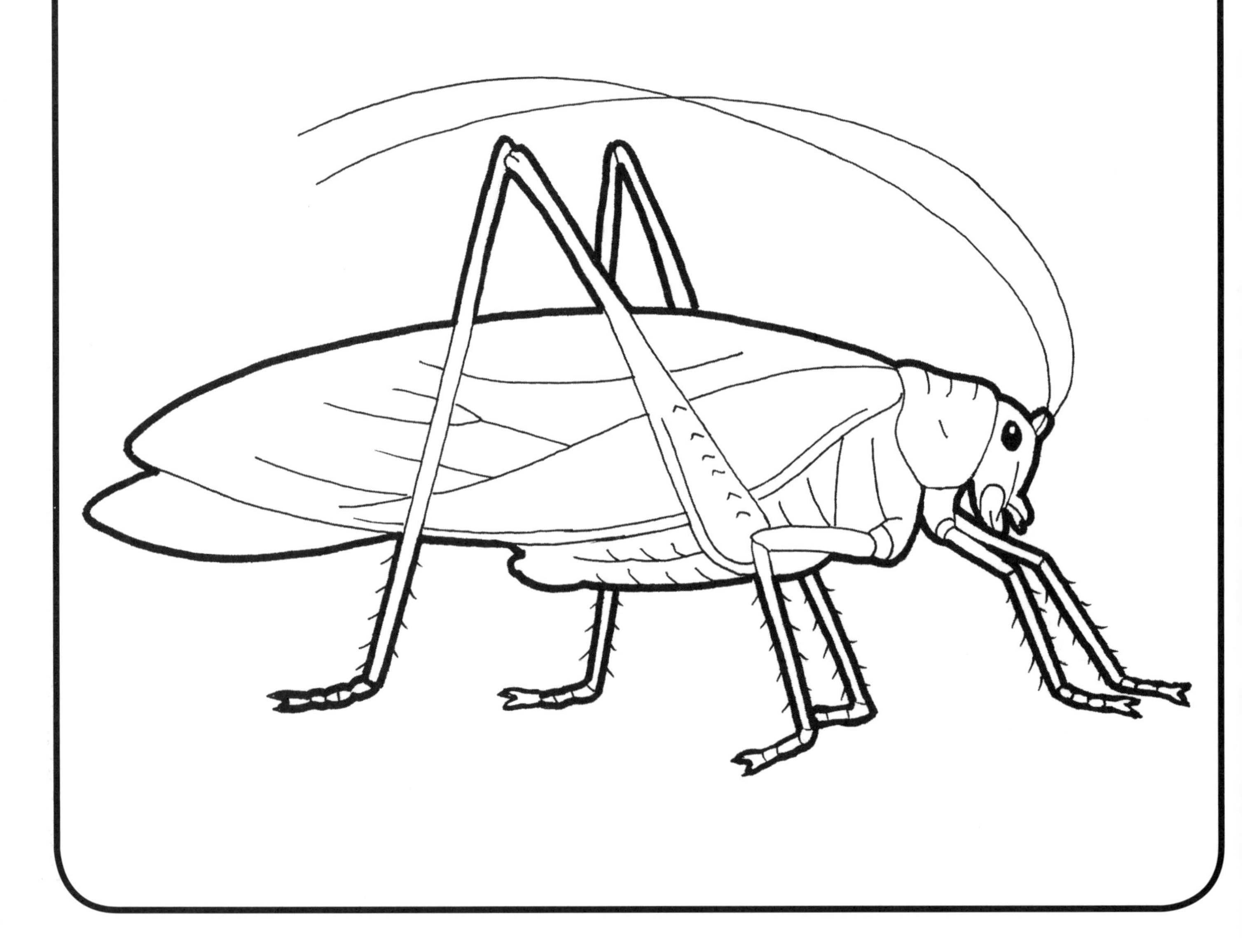

# Katydid

Sea slugs are among the most striking and colourful animals to be found in our waters. They crawl about on reefs looking for small plants and animals to eat – even jellyfish. Their bright colours are a warning to potential predators that the sea slug will make a very unpleasant meal.

# Blue and Yellow Sea Slug

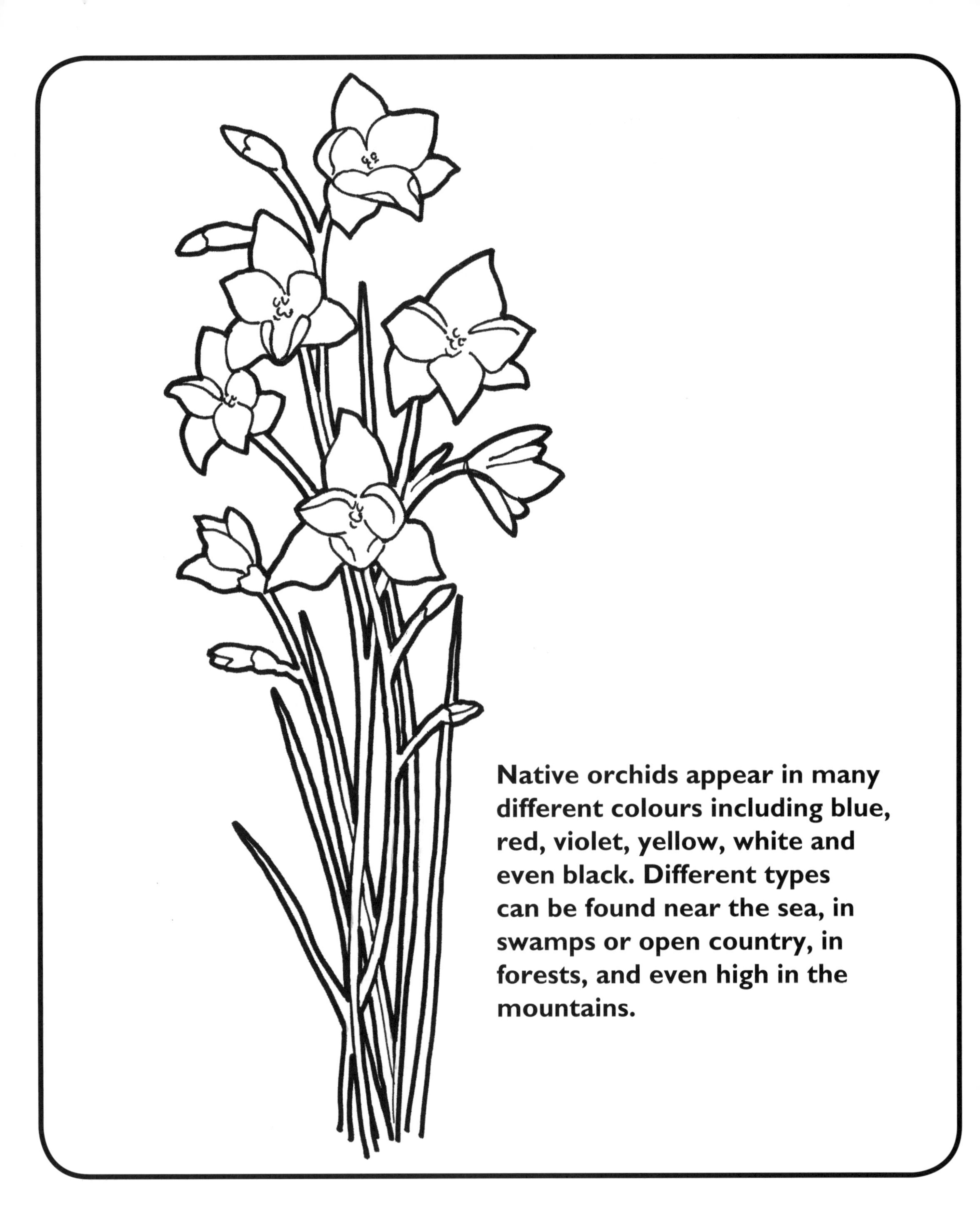

Native orchids appear in many different colours including blue, red, violet, yellow, white and even black. Different types can be found near the sea, in swamps or open country, in forests, and even high in the mountains.

# Blue Swamp Orchid

**Originally from Europe, this bird is found nationwide in gardens, orchards and farmlands, and is today more common here than in Britain. It eats insects and spiders, but mainly seeds of all kinds. During winter, goldfinches form large flocks in open countryside.**

# Goldfinch

# Laughing Owl

**In late summer, cicadas appear by the thousand and call in a great deafening chorus. The sound is made by the males drumming special body chambers, or by clapping their wings against a hard surface. The noise is made to attract a female to mate.**

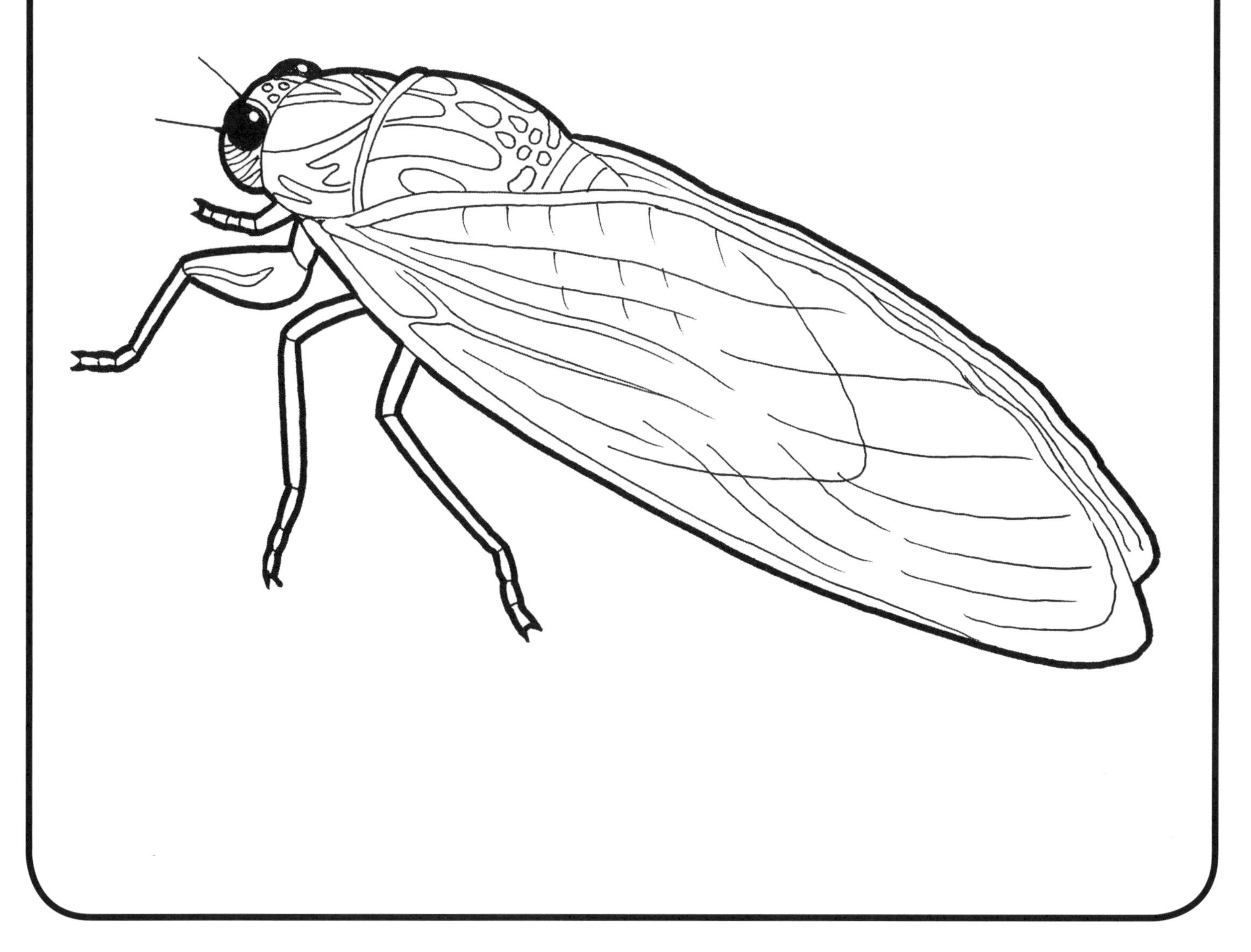

# Cicada

**A poor flyer, the kokako prefers to scramble and flutter from branch to branch as it seeks out fruit, flowers and insects to eat. It feeds rather like a parrot, standing on one foot and holding its food with the other while it takes a bite!**

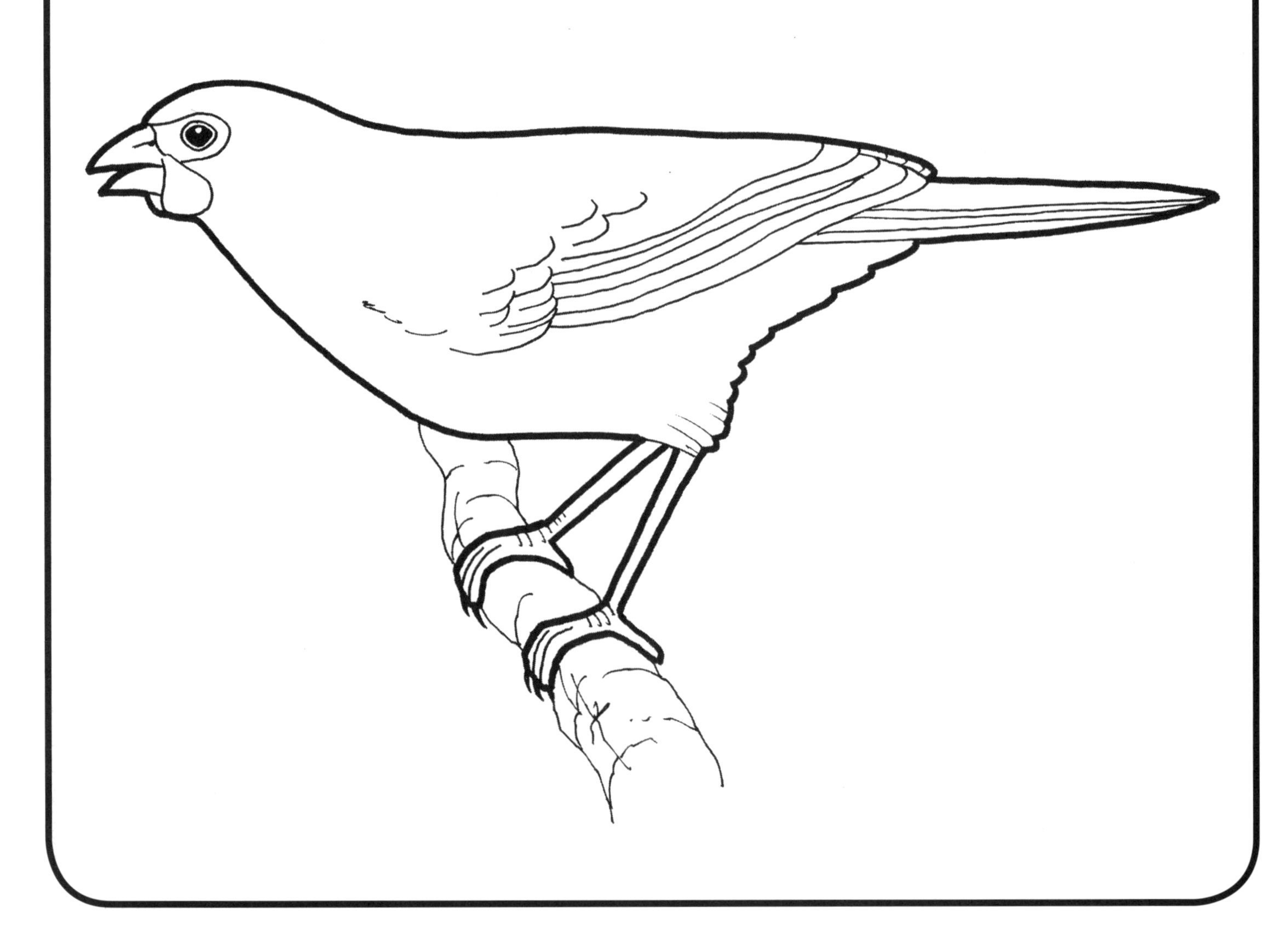

# Kokako

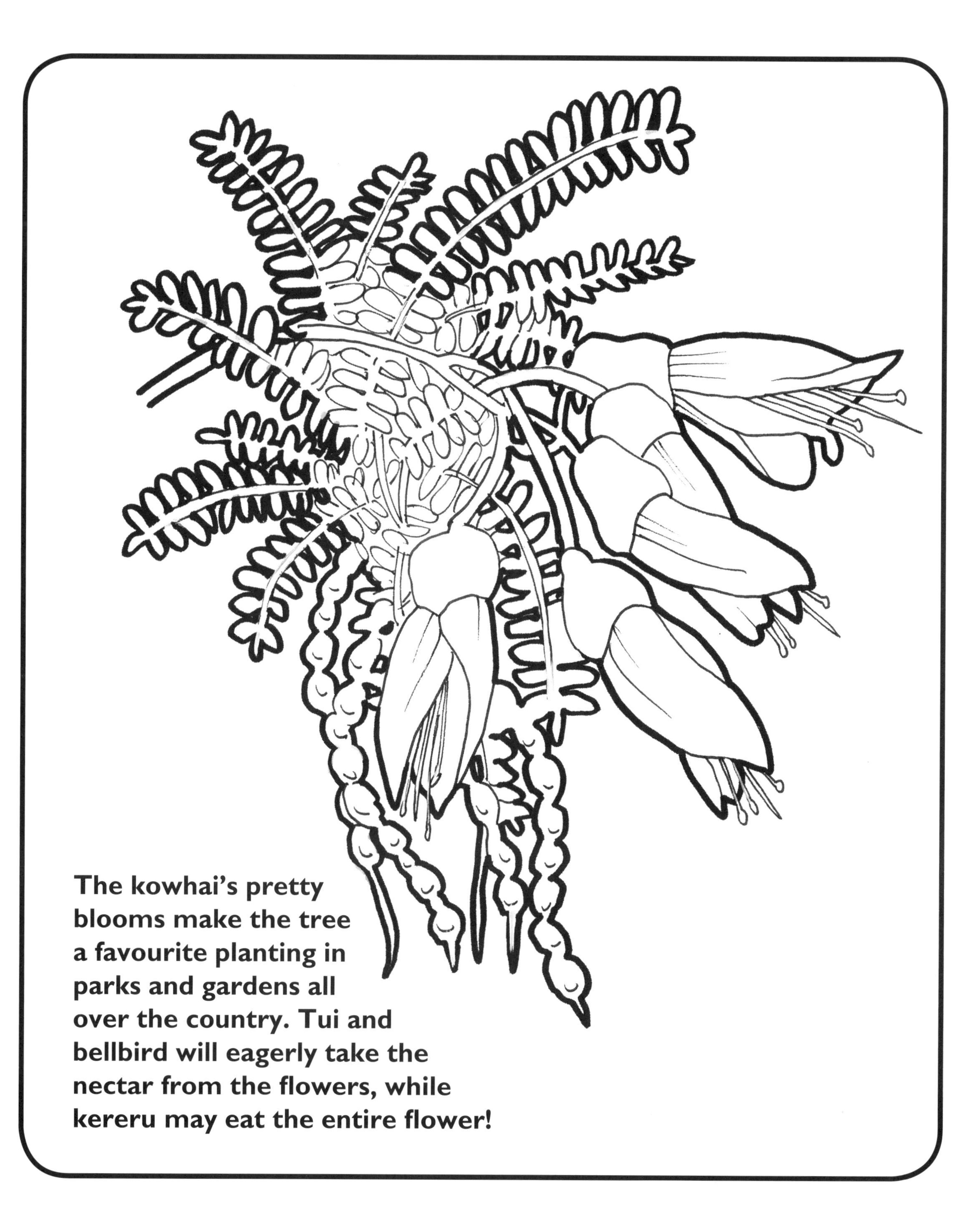

The kowhai's pretty blooms make the tree a favourite planting in parks and gardens all over the country. Tui and bellbird will eagerly take the nectar from the flowers, while kereru may eat the entire flower!

# Kowhai

Flying reptiles like this probably evolved about 70 million years before the first birds appeared. The New Zealand species had a wingspan of 3 to 4 metres, and it fed on fish and squid.

# Pterosaur

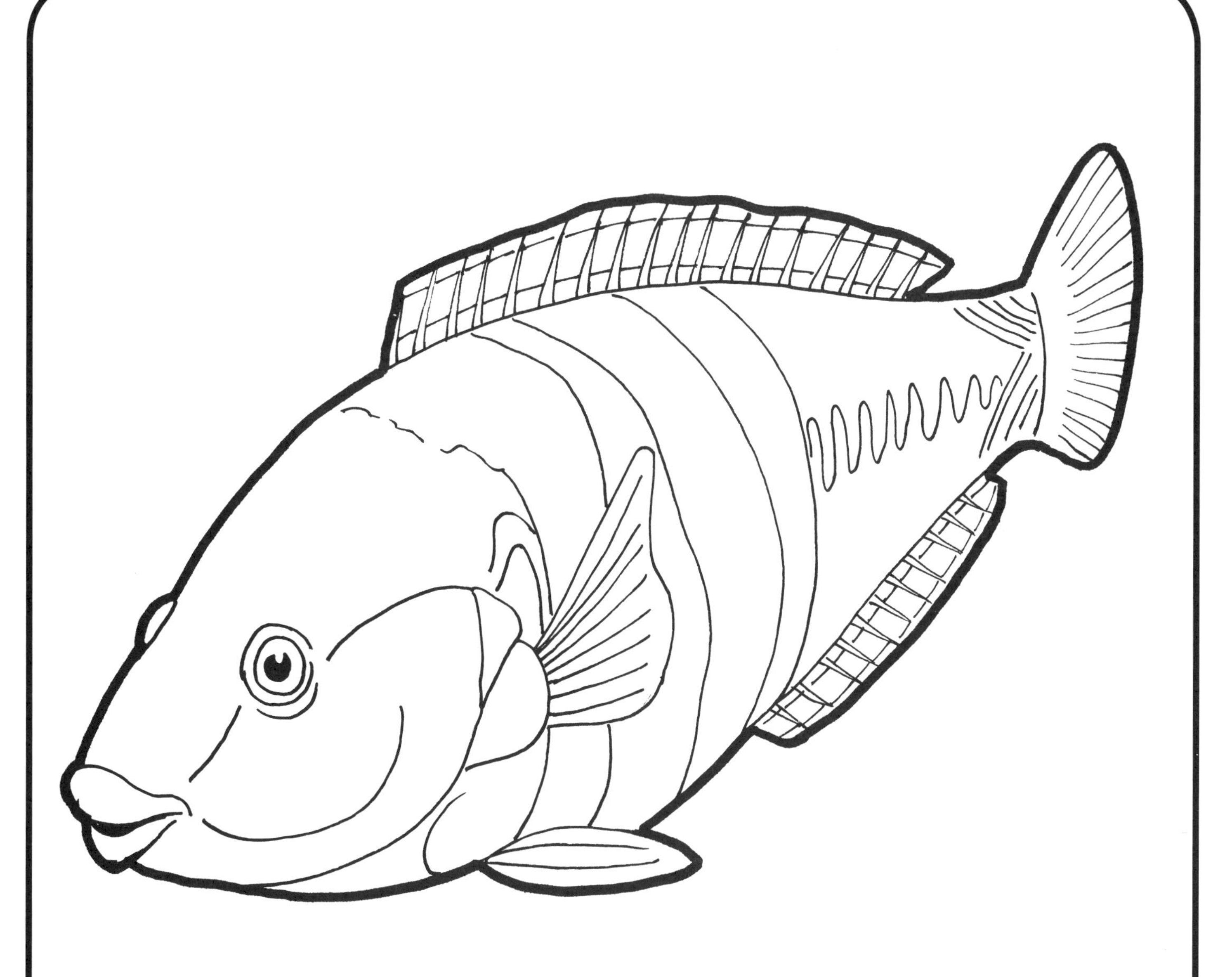

This very colourful fish is common around the reefs. It has large, well defined teeth. It feeds on worms, crustaceans, shellfish and sea urchins around the sea floor, and will overturn small rocks and stones to get at any prey that might be hiding underneath. After dark, it digs itself into the sand to remain hidden from any night-time predators.

# Sandager's Wrasse

The New Zealand pigeon lives in forests and likes to eat many different kinds of berries. Its feathers were once used by Maori to make cloaks.

# New Zealand Pigeon

**The rifleman is our smallest bird – it's just 8 centimetres from its bill to the tip of its tail – and it weighs less than a $1 coin. It picks off insects and spiders from forest tree trunks by walking and climbing up the tree like on a spiral staircase.**

# Rifleman

**This is one of our most common butterflies, and also one of the smallest. It enjoys warm and dry conditions. During the summer, it flies close to the ground in gardens all around the country. It can also be seen on roadsides and farmland, by the seashore, and in higher country.**

# Blue Butterfly

This little bird has a pretty 'trailing' song, but it's usually hard to see, since it likes to stay within the shade and protection of tree foliage. The warbler flies among the branches to snatch up insects and spiders to eat.

# Grey Warbler

**Haast's eagle was the largest bird of prey that the world has ever seen – its talons were the size of a tiger's. This eagle became extinct a few hundred years ago.**

# Haast's Eagle

Large marine reptiles swam in New Zealand seas hundreds of millions of years ago. They fed on small fish and squid, and had lots of small, sharp teeth for hunting. They were up to 9 metres long.

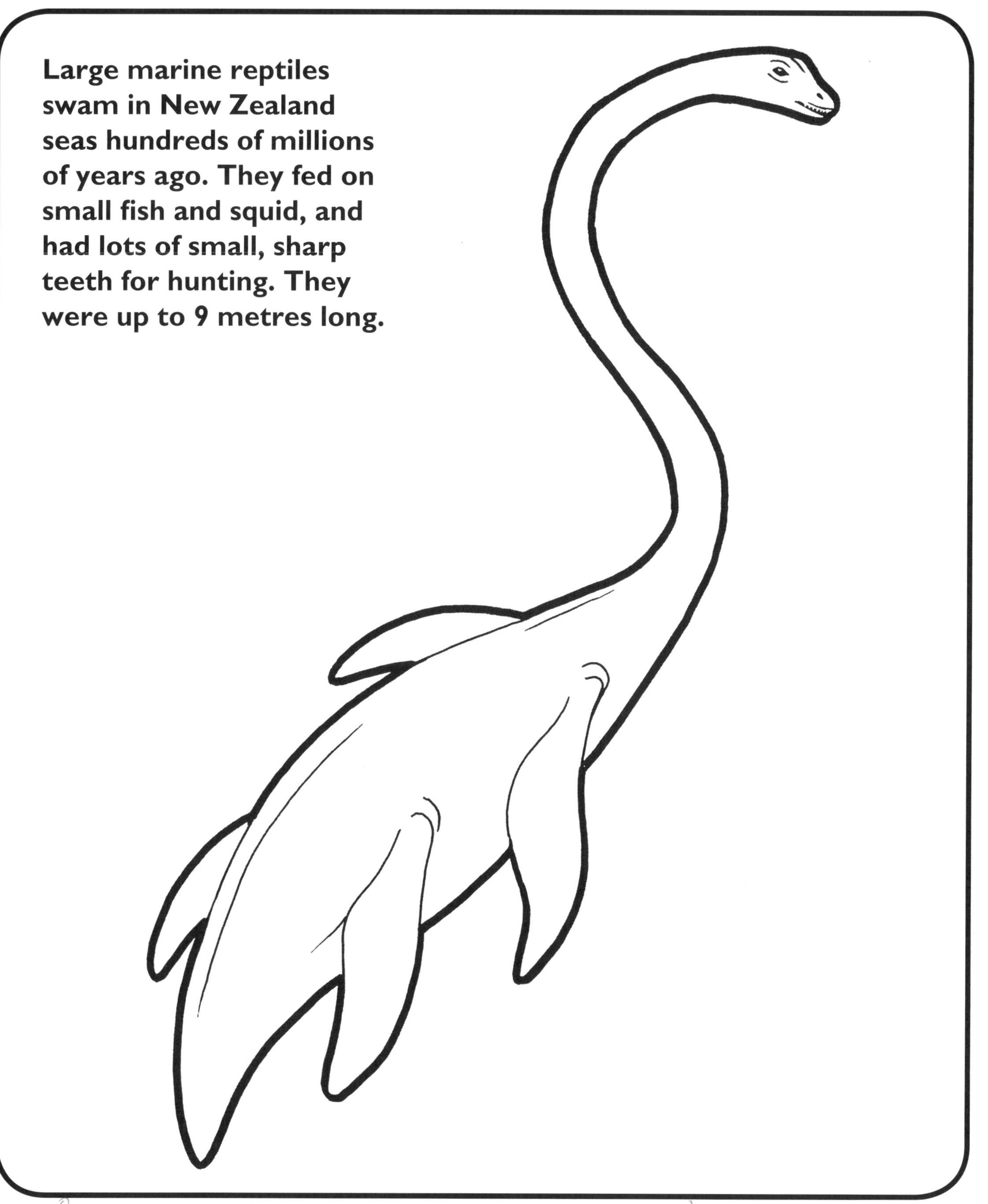

8 39 inches = 1 meter    7 x 12 = 84 + 6 = 90 inches
9
351 inches

# Elasmosaur

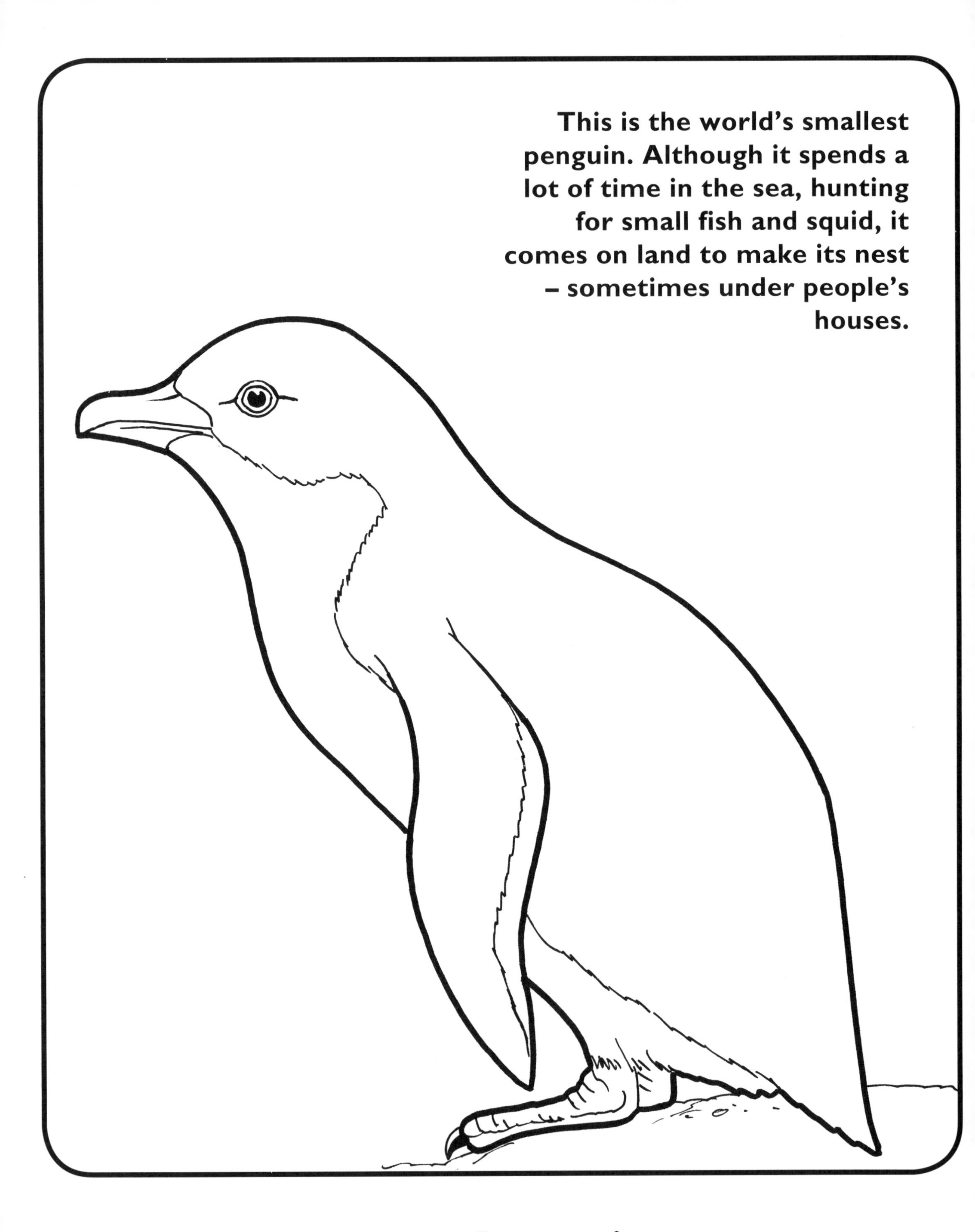

**This is the world's smallest penguin. Although it spends a lot of time in the sea, hunting for small fish and squid, it comes on land to make its nest – sometimes under people's houses.**

# Blue Penguin

**This seaside plant has thick, fleshy, three-sided leaves, and woody stems that grow in tangles along the ground. It is found growing close to the sea, usually just above the high-tide mark. The flowers turn to follow the sun during the day.**

# Maori Ice Plant

The little katipo lives in the tangle of old driftwood and grasses on sandy beaches, where it catches small insects for food. Though its venomous bite is harmful to humans, this spider is shy and will usually run away if disturbed.

# Katipo

**There are about 1000 species of these shells around the world, and nearly 100 can be found on sandy beaches on New Zealand coasts. The very pretty, 2-centimetre-wide wheel shell lives just under the surface at low tide, where it filters tiny food particles from the sand.**

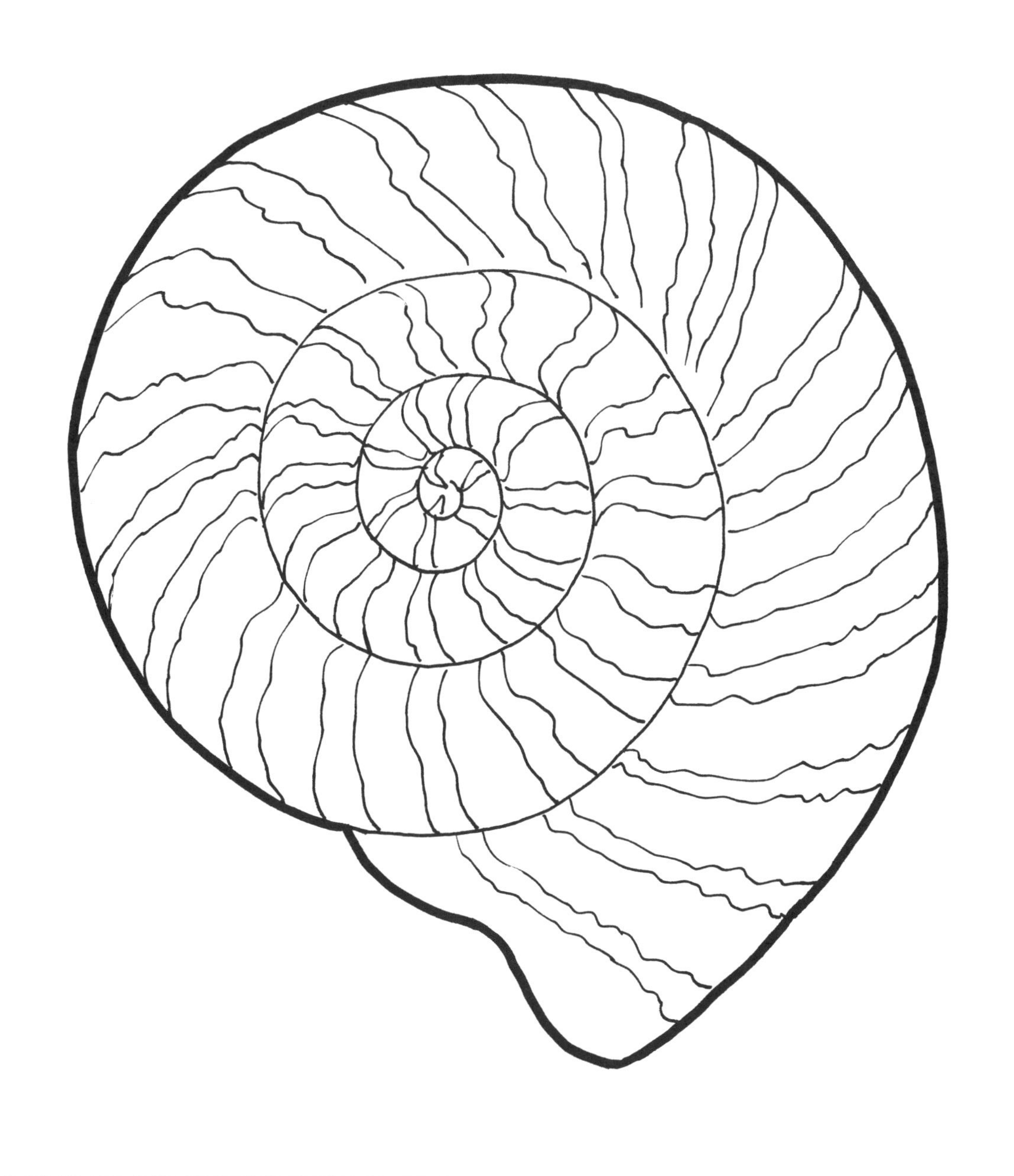

# Wheel Shell

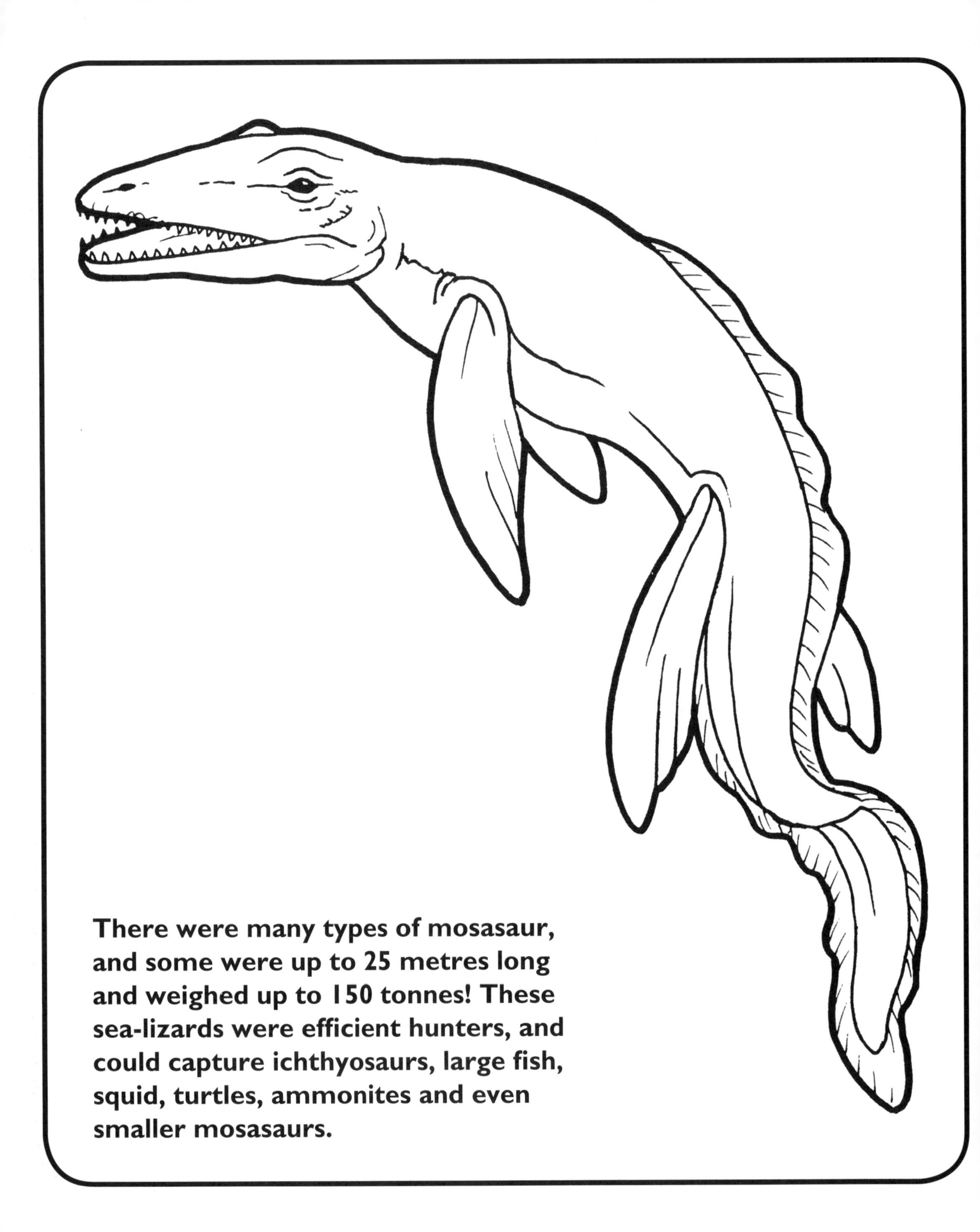

**There were many types of mosasaur, and some were up to 25 metres long and weighed up to 150 tonnes! These sea-lizards were efficient hunters, and could capture ichthyosaurs, large fish, squid, turtles, ammonites and even smaller mosasaurs.**

# Mosasaur

The little owl was brought to New Zealand in 1906 to help control the small birds that were eating farm crops, but the little owl much preferred to eat spiders and insects instead, and left the birds alone!

## Little Owl

The yellow-eyed penguin or hoiho may be the rarest of all the penguins, with a total population of around 5000 birds. It catches fish and squid in the sea, and can make dives as deep as 160 metres to find its prey. It nests mostly on the southern coasts of the South Island.

# Yellow-eyed Penguin

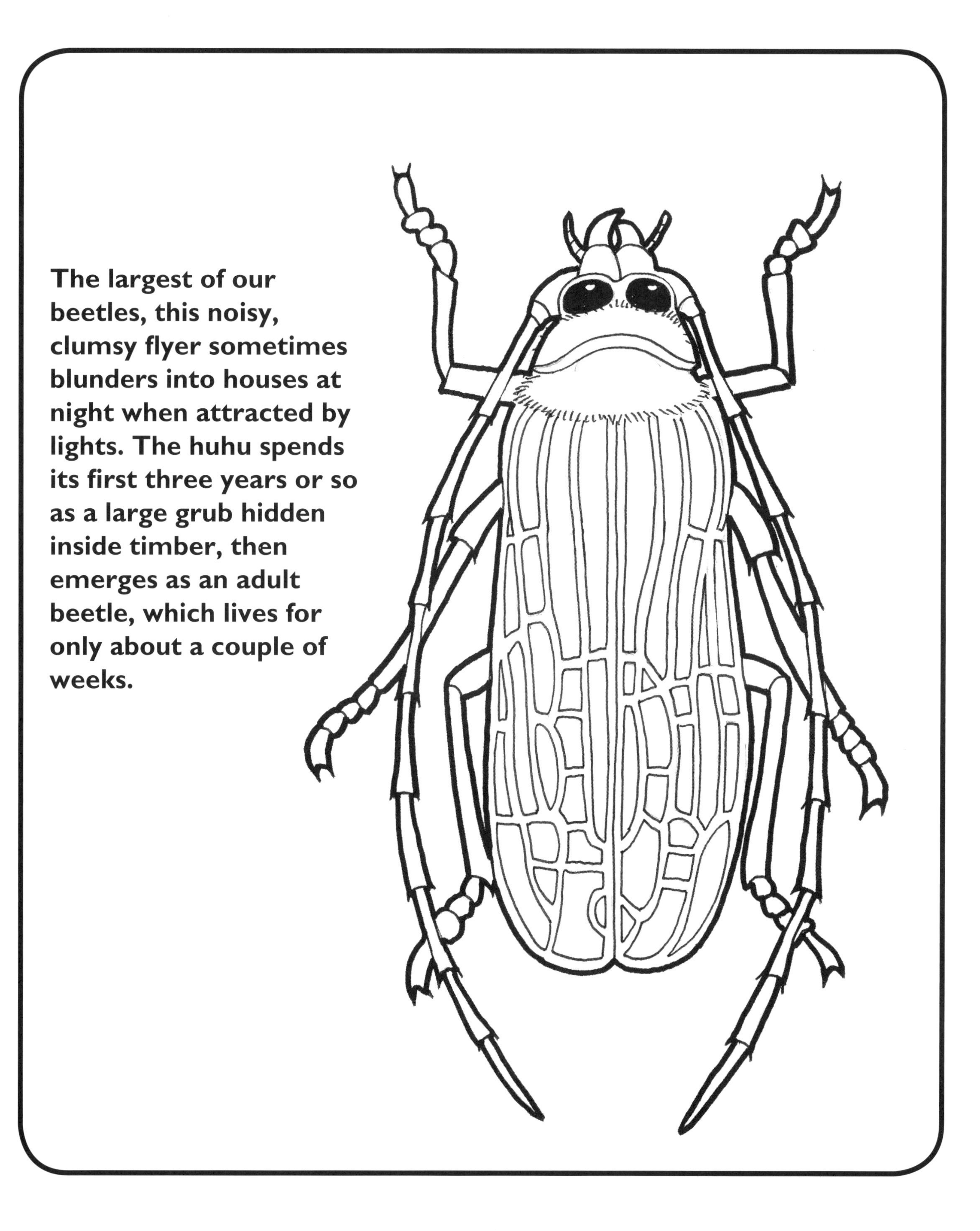

**The largest of our beetles, this noisy, clumsy flyer sometimes blunders into houses at night when attracted by lights. The huhu spends its first three years or so as a large grub hidden inside timber, then emerges as an adult beetle, which lives for only about a couple of weeks.**

# Huhu

**The snapper is not a fussy hunter – it will eat all sorts of small fish, crabs, sea urchins and worms. It has very well developed teeth, including molars and canines, that are strong enough to crunch through the toughest of prey – even the shells of limpets and other shellfish. It can live for up to 60 years.**

# Snapper

**This 12-centimetre shell has two halves: one rounded, and the other flat. The soft animal lives inside, and can open the two halves to feed or close them to hide. It can even 'flap' the two halves of the shell to swim through the water.**

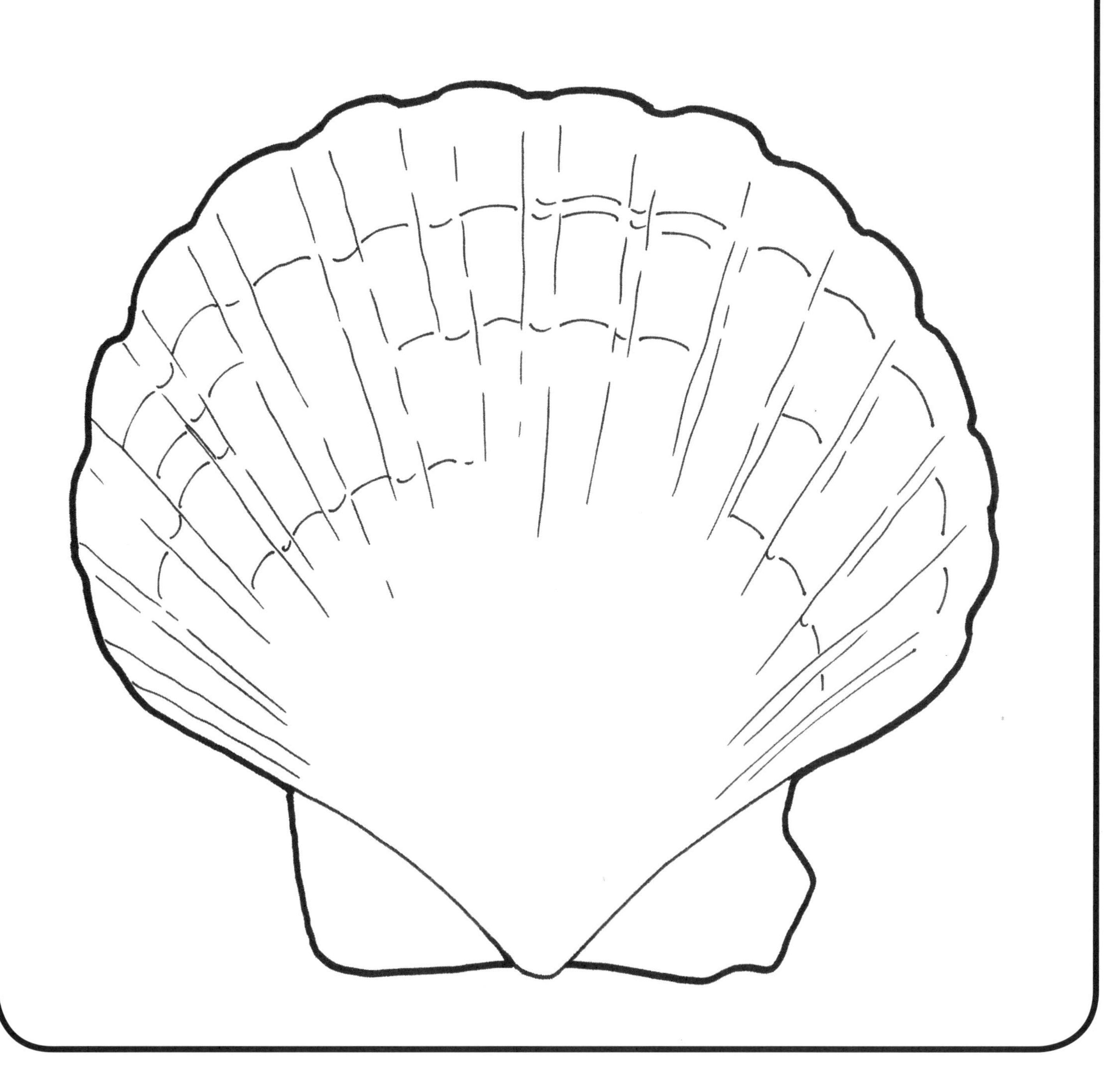

# Common Scallop

**Growing to around 4–12 metres in height, with masses of small pink or white flowers, manuka or tea-tree is one of our most attractive flowering trees. It is also useful: bees gather its pollen to produce manuka honey, and we use manuka to make tea-tree oil.**

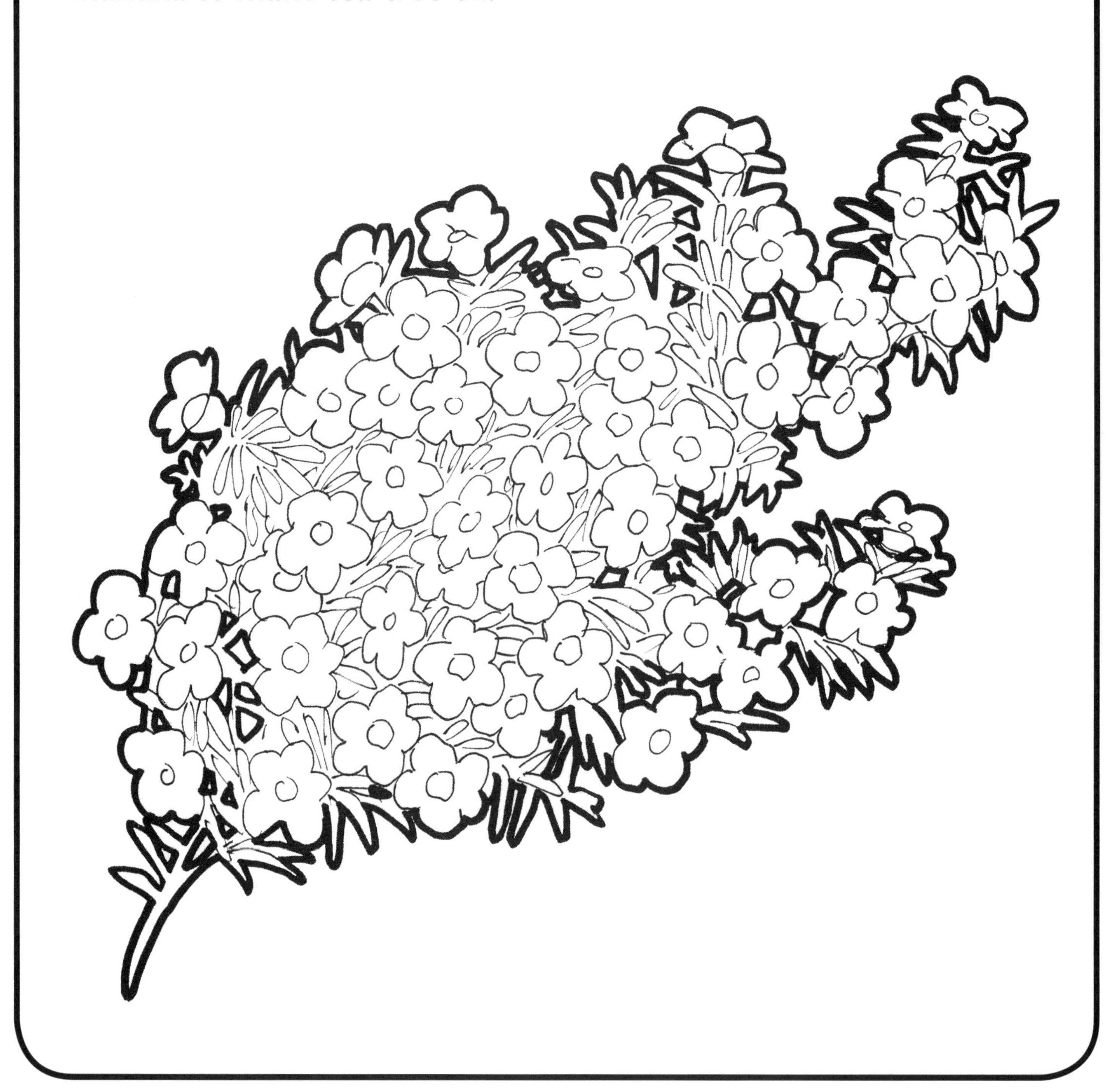

# Manuka

The silvereye has a tongue like a brush which helps it drink nectar from flowers. Silvereyes are also quick to eat bread or sugar water if you leave some in the garden.

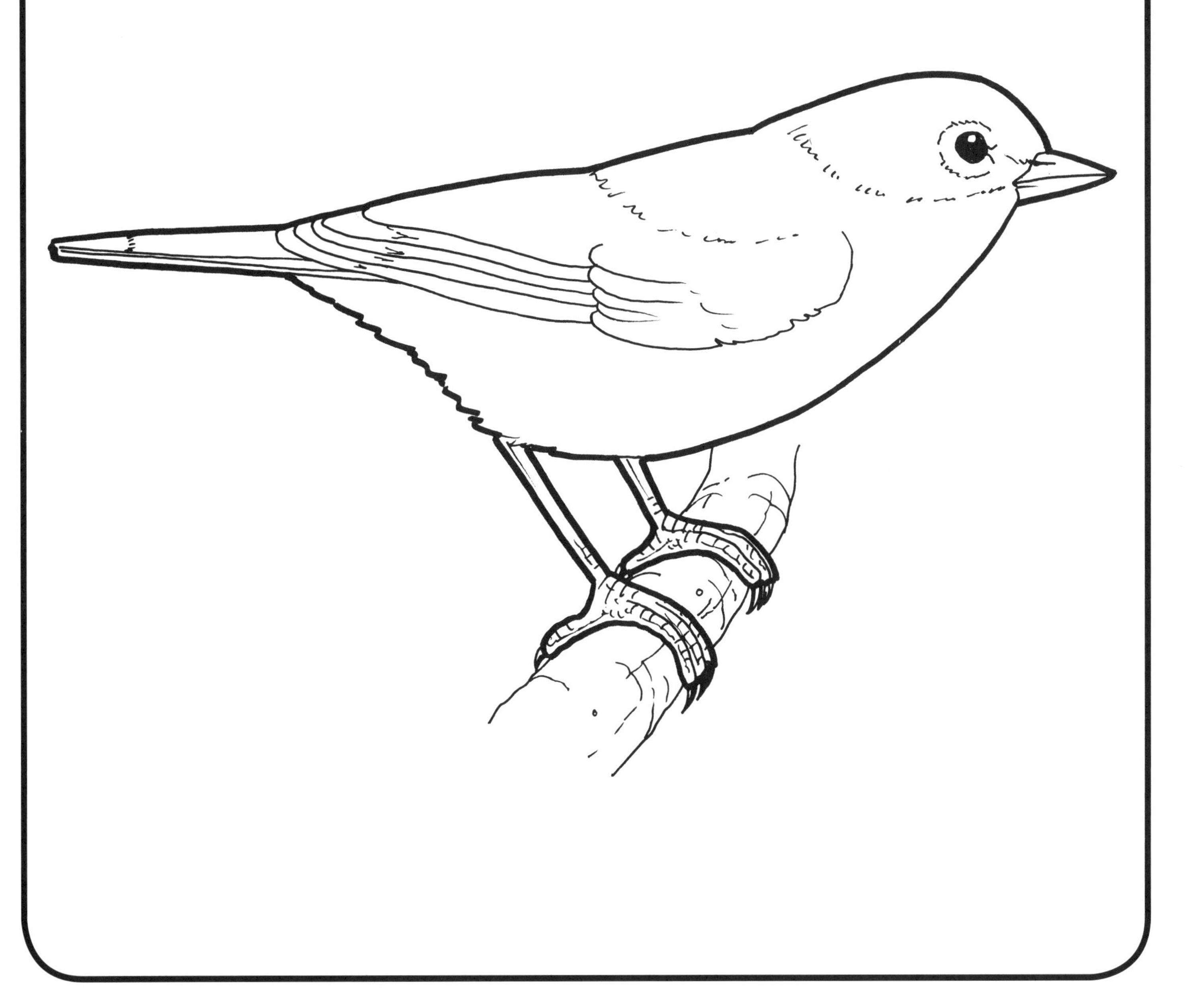

# Silvereye

# Extinct Amphibian

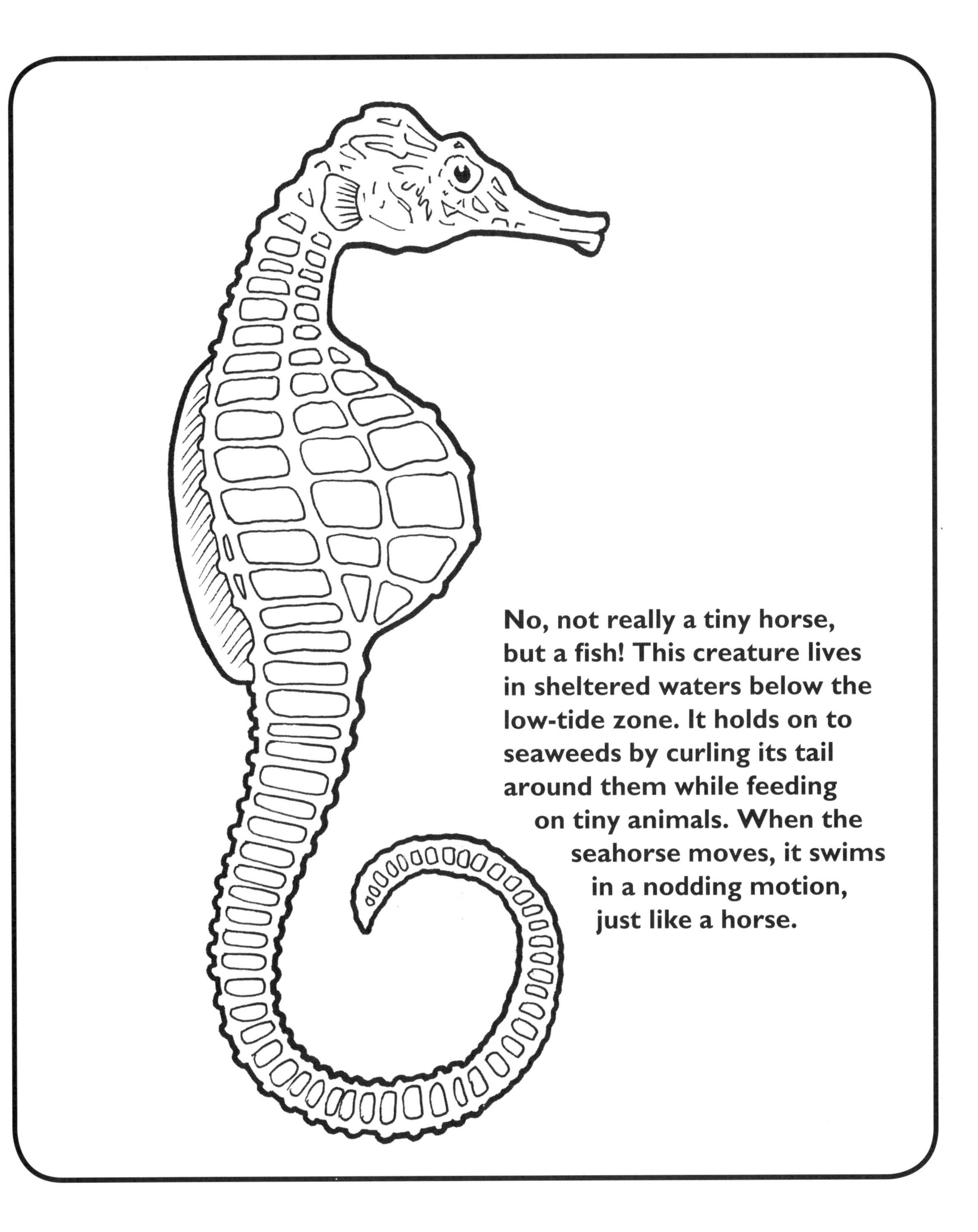

No, not really a tiny horse, but a fish! This creature lives in sheltered waters below the low-tide zone. It holds on to seaweeds by curling its tail around them while feeding on tiny animals. When the seahorse moves, it swims in a nodding motion, just like a horse.

## Seahorse

This was the smallest flightless bird in the world, weighing just 22 grams, about the same as a two-dollar coin! Rats, dogs and cats were a threat for tiny birds like this, and it became extinct by 1875.

## Lyall's Wren

This is one of the more common sea stars to be seen around northern reefs. Most sea stars are covered in spines but the firebrick star is covered in lots of small knobs and lumps. Using many tiny tube feet, it crawls around the reefs to seek out small animals of all kinds to eat, especially sponges.

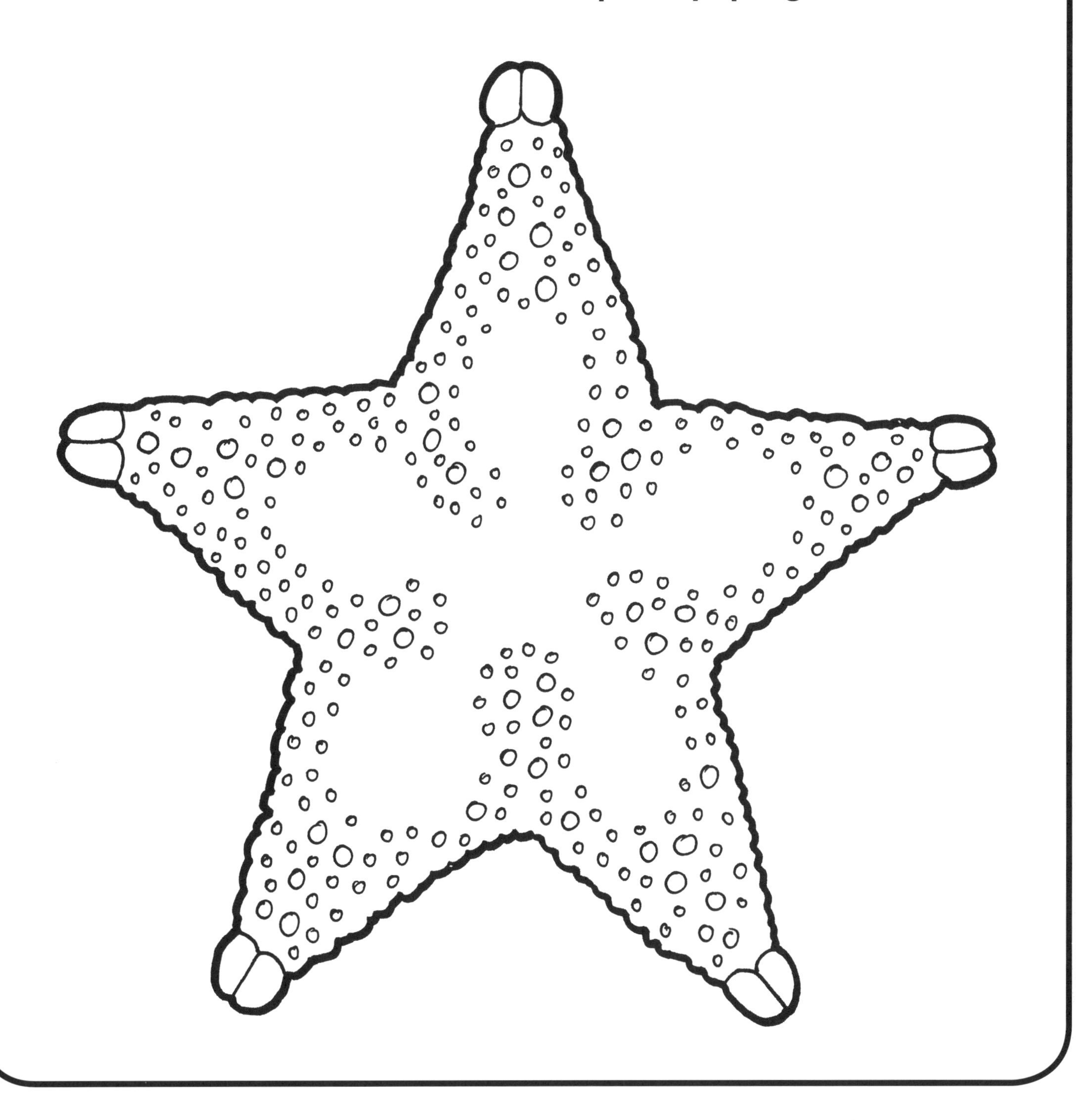

# Firebrick Star

# Eastern Rosella

**This bird is named after the 'saddle' of orange-brown feathers across its back. It likes to rummage in leaf litter on the forest floor, looking for insects or spiders to eat, or to dig at rotten wood with its strong beak in order to get at grubs.**

# Saddleback

You may find this large insect in your garden, since it likes to hide in stacks of firewood or under old leaves. Weta come out in the evening to look for food such as small insects and leaves, and they are sometimes eaten by birds and rats.

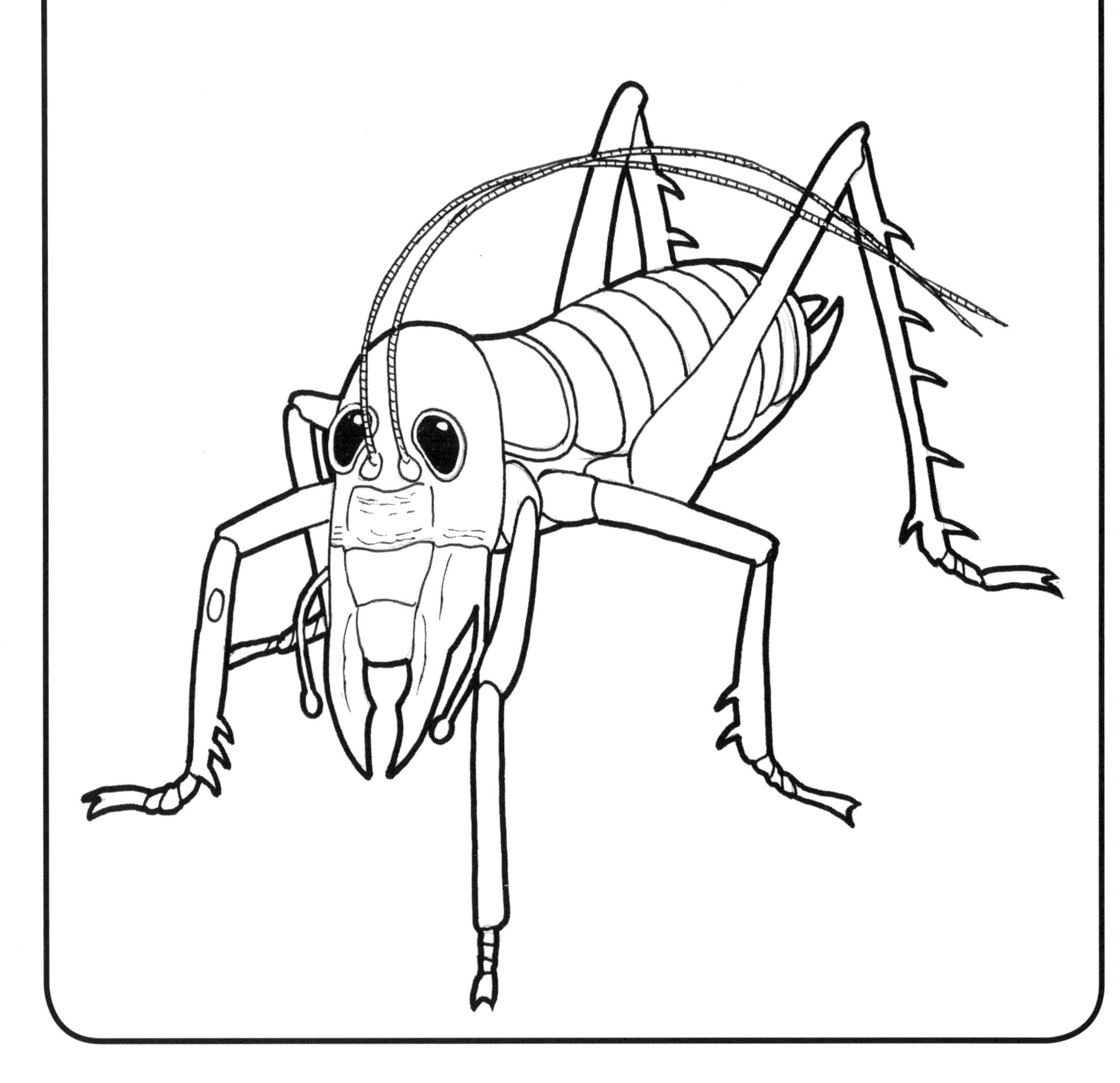

## Tree Weta

Yellow-Crowned Parakeet
Page 2
Bumble-bee
Page 3
Kingfisher
Page 4
Green Gecko
Page 5
Lord Howe Coralfish
Page 9
Kiwi
Page 6
Sauropod
Page 8
Pohutukawa
Page 7

Tui
Page 11
Giant Dragonfly
Page 10
Katydid
Page 14
Goldfinch
Page 17
Extinct Giant Penguin
Page 13
Blue Swamp
Orchid
Page 16
Moa
Page 12
Blue and Yellow
Sea Slug
Page 15

Kokako
Page 20
Laughing Owl
Page 18
Pterosaur
Page 22
Cicada
Page 19
Sandager's
Wrasse
Page 23
New Zealand
Pigeon
Page 24
Kowhai
Page 21
Rifleman
Page 25

Grey Warbler
Page 27
Haast's Eagle
Page 28
Blue Butterfly
Page 26
Blue Penguin
Page 30
Wheel Shell
Page 33
Elasmosaur
Page 29
Katipo
Page 32
Maori Ice Plant
Page 31

Yellow-eyed Penguin
Page 36
Huhu
Page 37
Mosasaur
Page 34
Little Owl
Page 35
Snapper
Page 38
Silvereye
Page 41
Manuka
Page 40
Common Scallop
Page 39

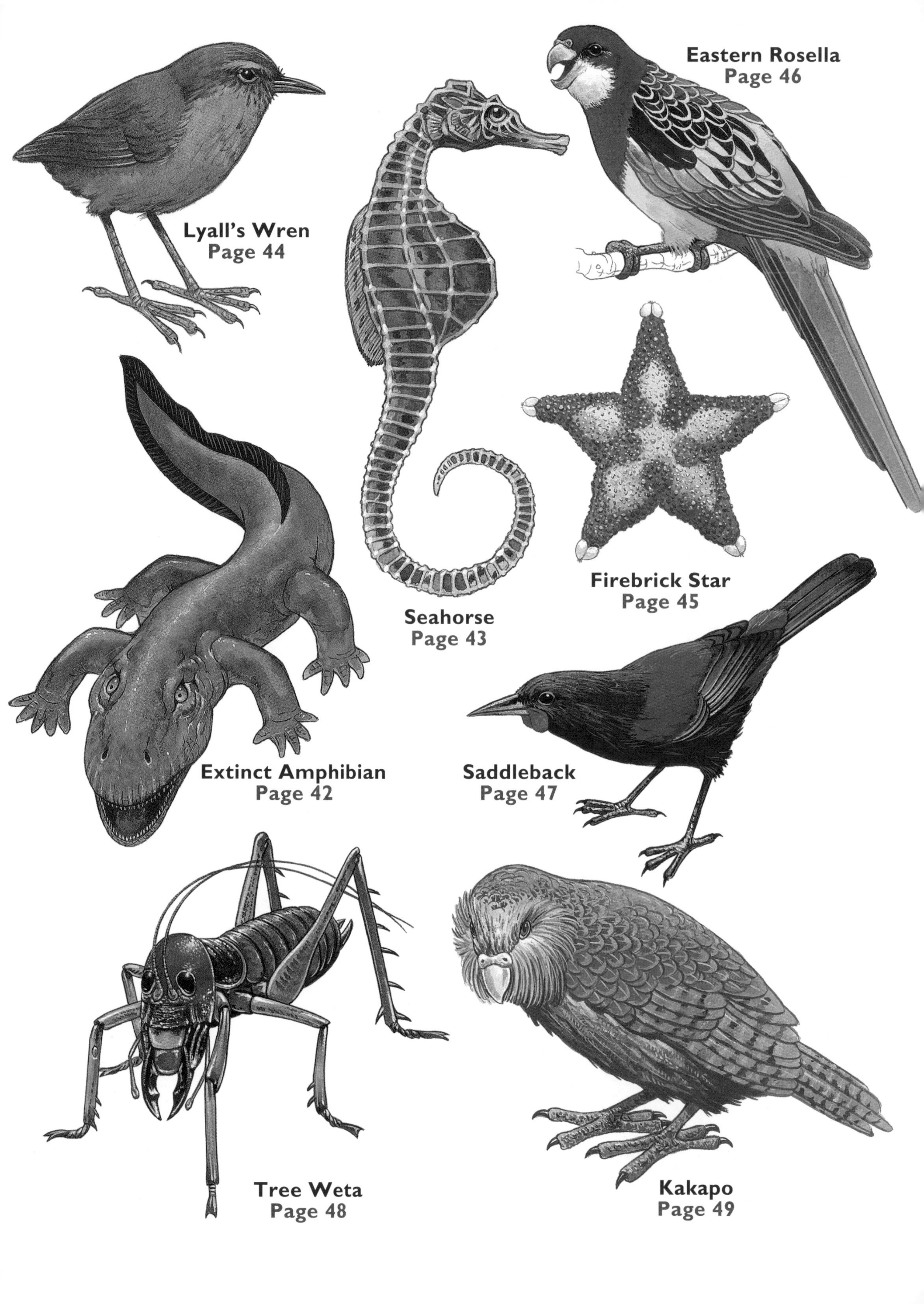
Lyall's Wren
Page 44
Eastern Rosella
Page 46
Firebrick Star
Page 45
Seahorse
Page 43
Extinct Amphibian
Page 42
Saddleback
Page 47
Tree Weta
Page 48
Kakapo
Page 49

Takahe
Page 50
Tiger Moth
Page 51
Extinct Giant Crab
Page 52
Orange Roughy
Page 53
False-toothed
Pelican
Page 54
Kaka
Page 55
Yellowhammer
Page 56
Common Skink
Page 57

Stitchbird
Page 64
Kea
Page 63
Extinct Giant Gecko
Page 65
Puriri Moth
Page 59
John Dory
Page 60
Clematis
Page 58
Crested Moa
Page 62
Camouflaged
Anemone
Page 61

Red Admiral
Butterfly
Page 66
Red-Billed Gull
Page 71
Megalosaur
Page 68
Ladybird
Page 67
Starling
Page 72
New Zealand
Falcon
Page 69
Ichthyosaur
Page 70
Paua
Page 73

Shining Cuckoo
Page 75
Yellow-bellied Sea Snake
Page 77
Weka
Page 79
Waitomo Frog
Page 74
Mudflat Top Shell
Page 80
Pliosaur
Page 78
Morepork
Page 76

Australasian Harrier
Page 81
Common Rock Crab
Page 82
Pukeko
Page 84
Nautilus
Page 83
Adzebill
Page 86
Praying Mantis
Page 88
Bellbird
Page 87
Ankylosaur
Page 85

Monarch Butterfly
Page 89
Extinct Land Mammal
Page 91
Chaffinch
Page 92
Allosaur
Page 95
Fantail
Page 94
Pied Oystercatcher
Page 90
Great White Shark
Page 93

**The kakapo is the world's heaviest parrot, and can live for up to 40 years. Its name means 'night parrot' because it prefers to hide away during the day, and then comes out to look for plant roots, leaves and seeds to eat during the night-time.**

# Kakapo

**Takahe can weigh up to 3 kilograms, and cannot fly. They were once thought to be extinct, but a small group was found in a South Island valley in 1948. Today you can see them in wildlife parks, where they are protected.**

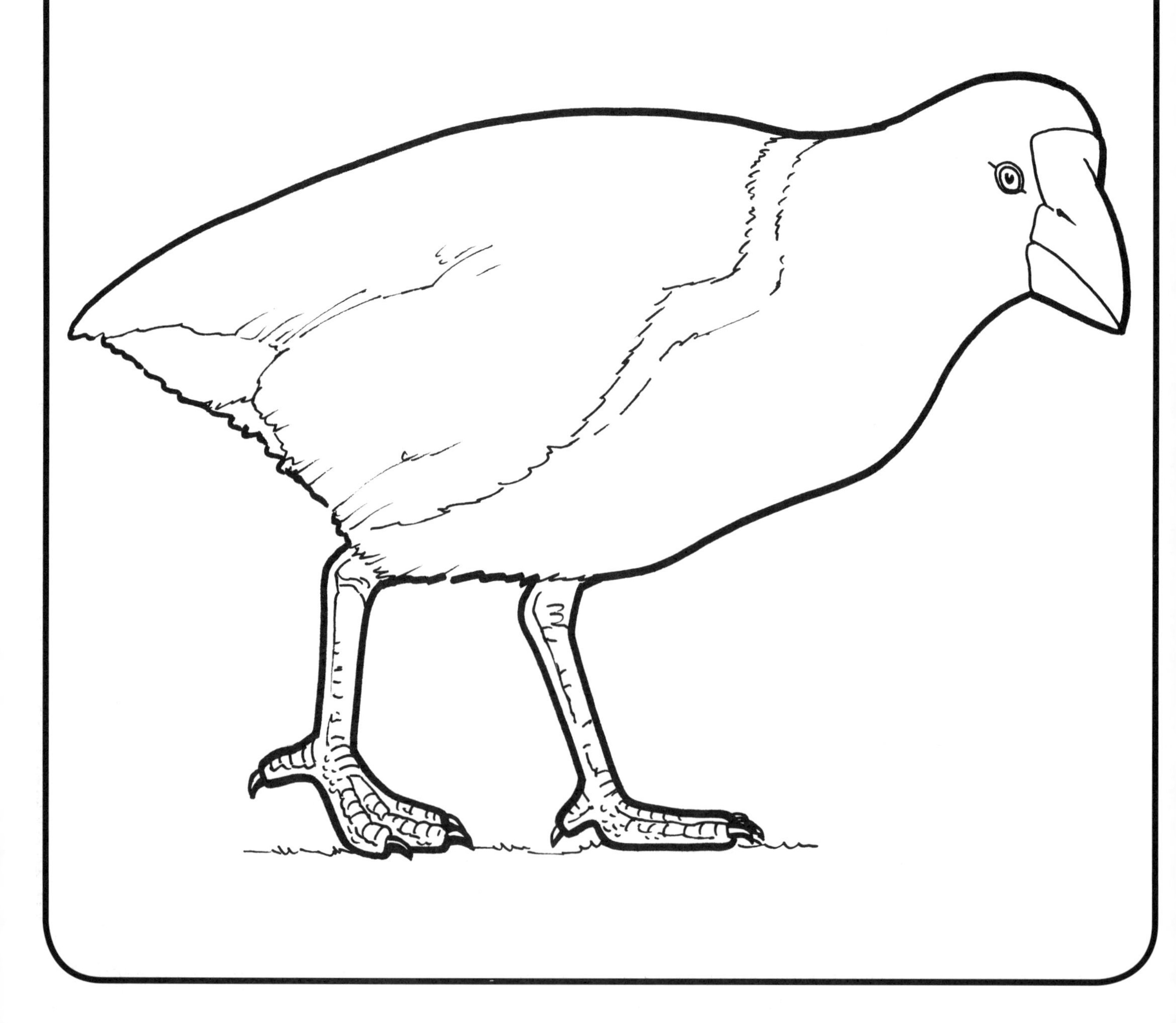

# Takahe

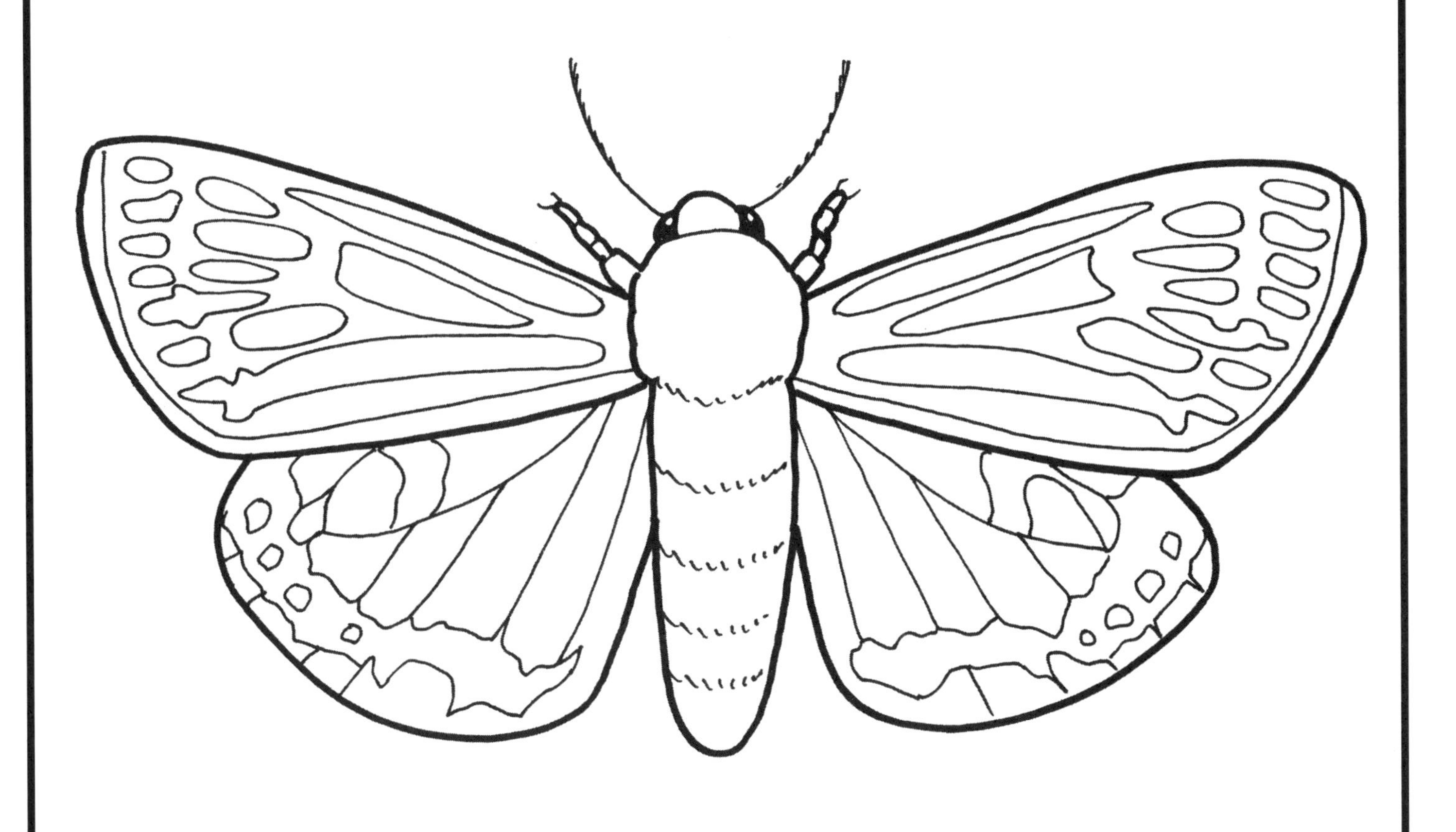

**It's easy to see how this moth gets its name: it's striped like a tiger! There are about eight species of tiger moth in New Zealand. Moths usually rest in the daytime and fly at night, but tiger moths can be seen during the day, zipping about low over open ground.**

# Tiger Moth

**Large crabs like this lived around New Zealand about 20 to 40 million years ago. The giant crab's body was over 14 centimetres across, and its large right claw was even bigger. It fed on seaside plants, small animals and even other crabs.**

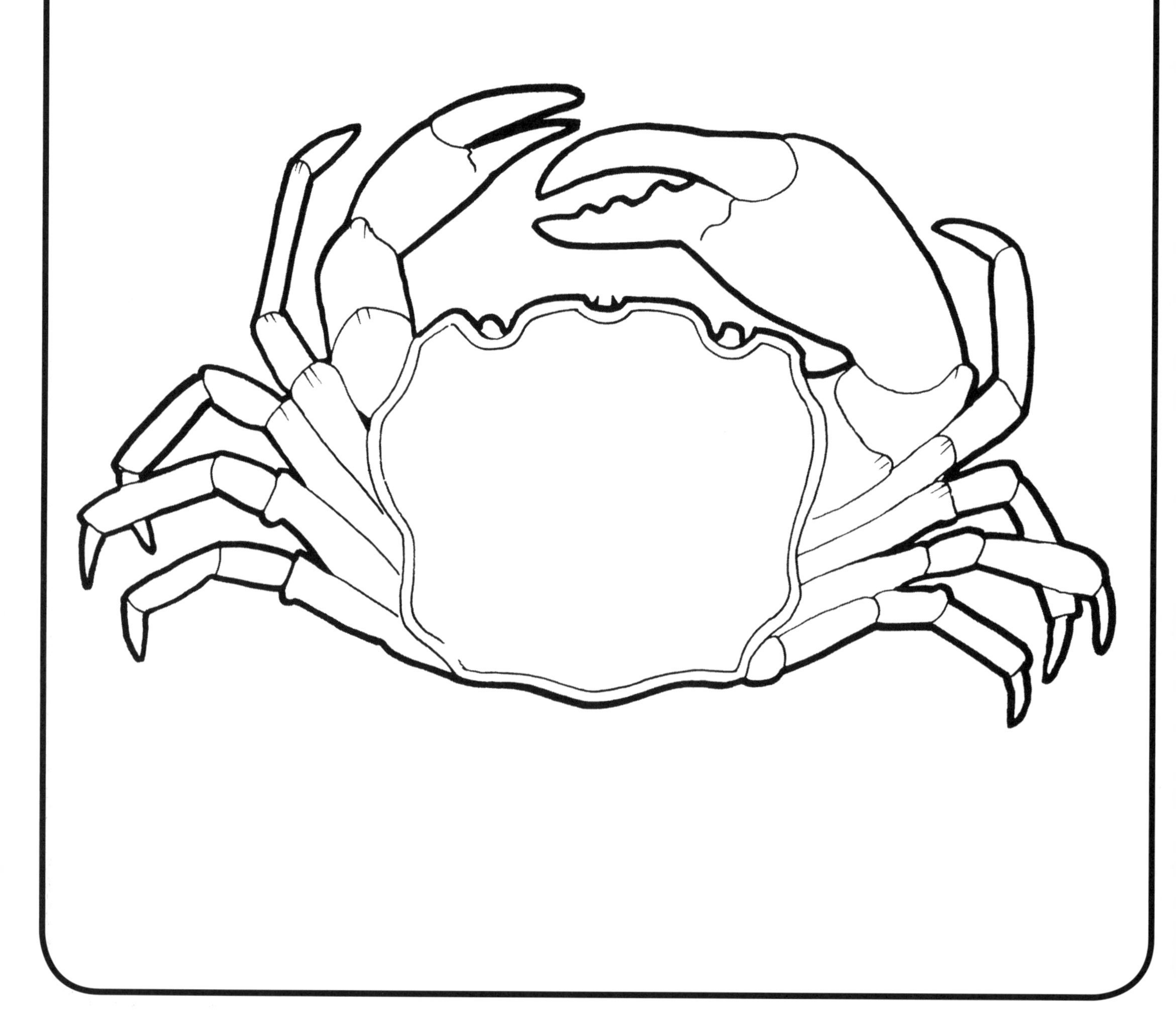

# Extinct Giant Crab

**This fish lives deep in the sea where there is practically no light at all. But the orange roughy has no problem finding food – it just hunts down those small fish, squid and shrimps that have organs that light up their bodies, making them easy to see in the gloom. Orange roughy can live for up to 150 years!**

# Orange Roughy

The largest of these birds had a wingspan of up to 5.5 metres. They didn't have any teeth, but the edges of their bills had sharply jagged points. They snatched prey – such as fish and squid – as they glided over the sea's surface.

# False-toothed Pelican

The kaka is a close relative of the kea, a mountain bird. The kaka is mostly a bird of the forests, where it climbs up and down trees to search out insects and their grubs, fruits, leaves and flower nectar.

# Kaka

**Yellowhammers were brought to New Zealand in the 1860s, and can now be found all over the country. Their song sounds very like 'a little bit of bread and no cheese'.**

# Yellowhammer

The common skink is one of several skink species found in gardens and parks around the country. Most eat small insects and spiders, as well as soft fruits. If disturbed by a predator, it can break off its tail, which continues to twitch while the skink makes its escape.

# Common Skink

**Clematis is a vine that climbs and grows on other plants and trees, such as manuka. The large, white flowers are very sweet-smelling, and each one measures up to 8 centimetres across. There are several species of clematis and they can live for up to a century.**

# Clematis

**With a wingspan of up to 15 centimetres, the puriri moth is the largest of our flying insects. It lives as a caterpillar in holes bored in North Island tree trunks for about seven years, and then as a flying adult for just a few days. The pattern and colour of its wings may vary greatly.**

# Puriri Moth

When hunting for food, such as small fish, the John dory can suddenly shoot its mouth out into a long tube shape to snatch up its surprised victim. This fish can also change its colour patterns to blend in with its surroundings as it glides slowly along in search of prey.

# John Dory

Although it looks like a garden flower, a sea anemone is actually an animal. Its arms are covered in tiny stinging cells which can stun and capture little animals in the water. The camouflaged anemone lives in the bottom of rock pools, where the sand, stones and pieces of broken shell help to disguise it.

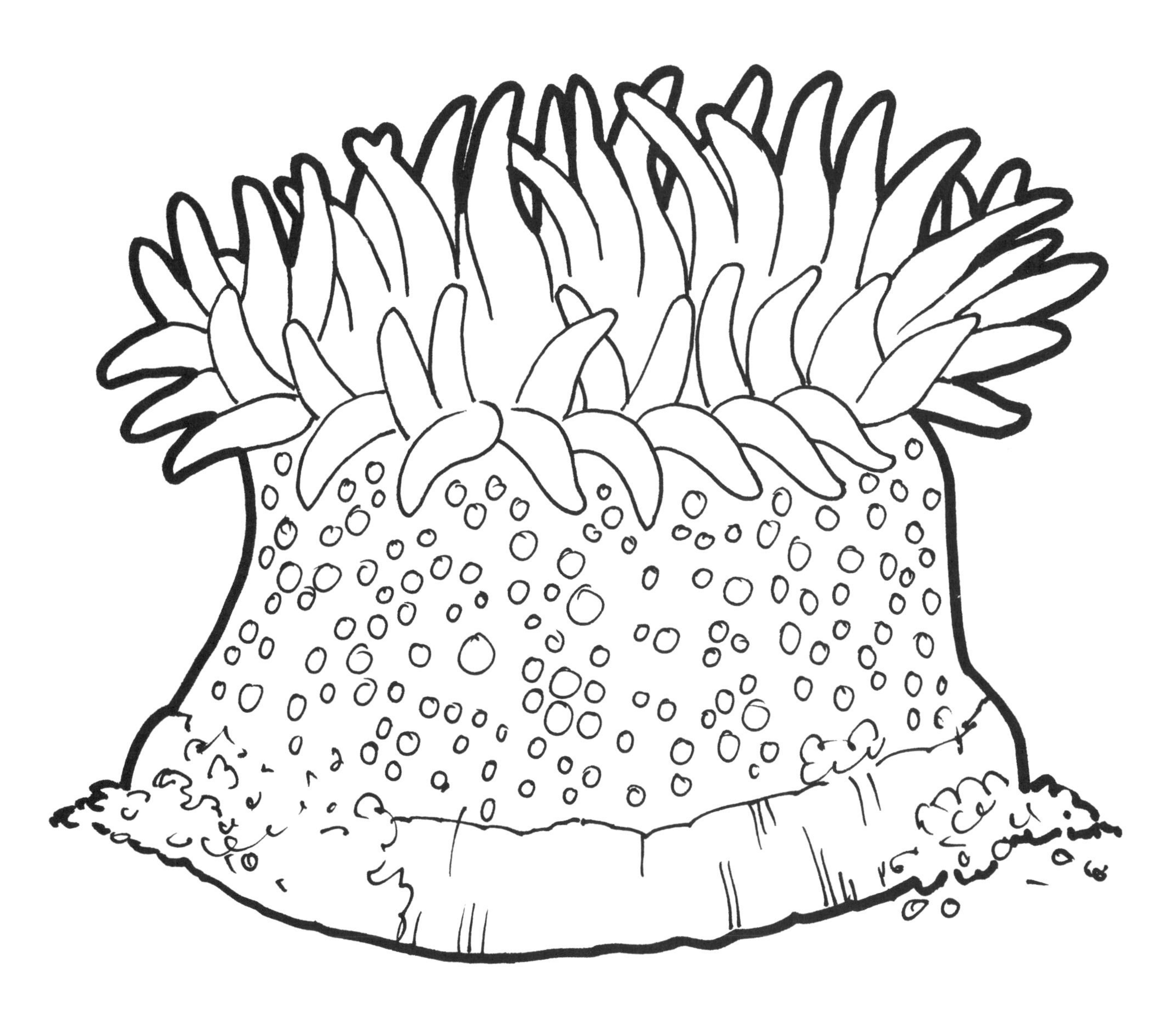

# Camouflaged Anemone

No one knows for certain what colours moa feathers were. Some species might have been brightly coloured – yellow, red, purple, black and white feathers have been found. Some moa species had crests of feathers on their heads, like this one!

# Crested Moa

The kea is a parrot that lives
in the mountains of the South
Island. It's a very clever and
mischievous bird, and will visit
campsites to see what it might
be able to eat or play with.

# Kea

**Like the bellbird and the tui, the stitchbird uses its brush-like tongue to feed on the nectar in flowers. Its Maori name, hihi, sounds like its call, which Europeans thought sounded like the English word 'stitch'.**

# Stitchbird

**At an overall length of 62 centimetres (larger than a tuatara) this was the biggest gecko ever to have lived. Also known as kawekaweau, the giant gecko was last seen in 1870.**

# Extinct Giant Gecko

**About five admiral butterfly species can be found around New Zealand, all with similar markings, though with different colour patterns. Most are also found in Australia, but the red admiral lives only in New Zealand. Its Maori name of kahukura means 'red cloak'.**

# Red Admiral Butterfly

**Ladybirds are beetles, and there are about 40 different types in New Zealand, in a variety of colours and with different numbers of spots. Ladybirds are the gardener's friend: they eat aphids and help to keep plants free of these little pests.**

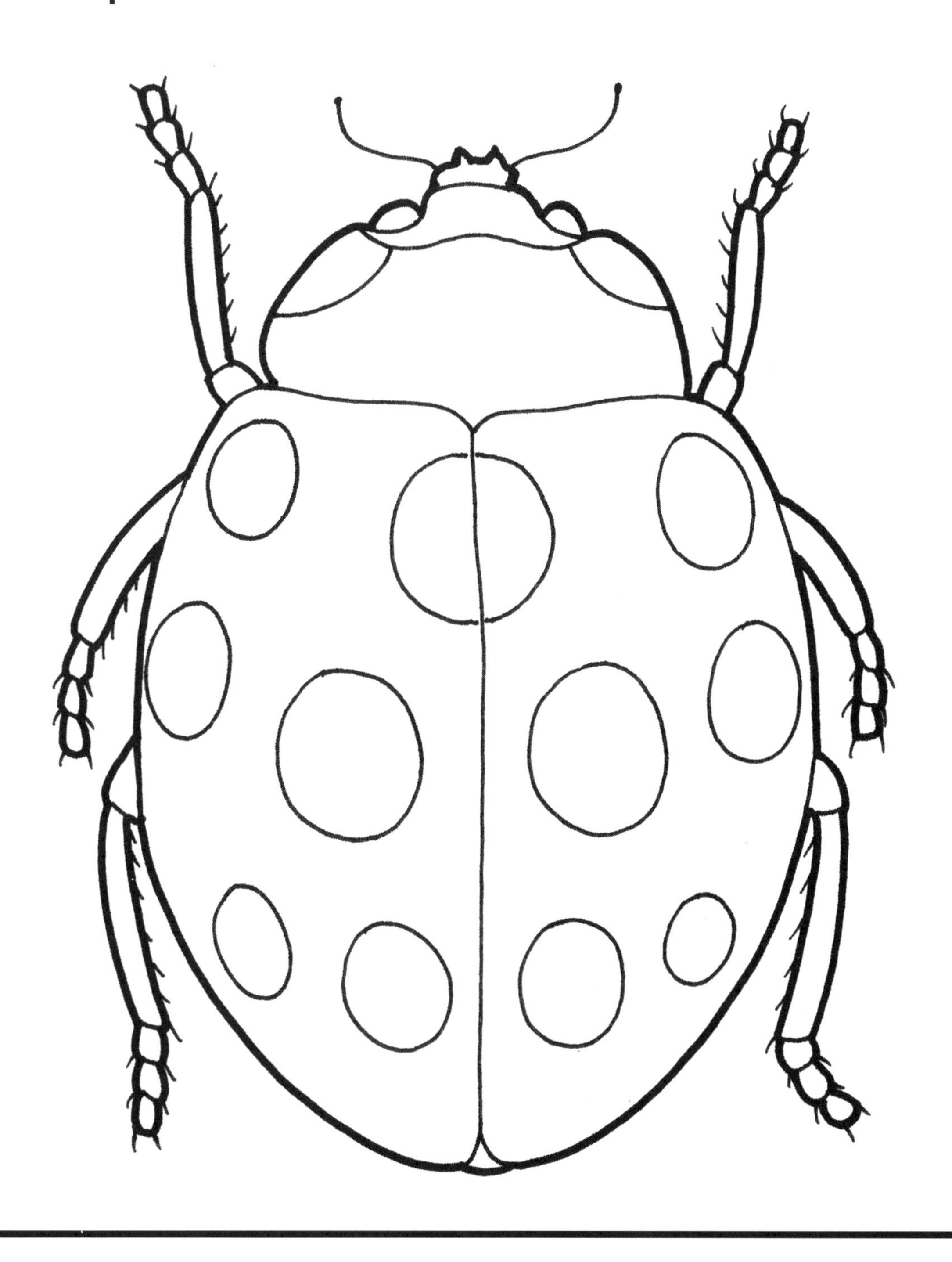

# Ladybird

This dinosaur was one of the very first types to be identified, in England, in the 1870s. Measuring 4 metres long, its name means ‘great lizard’, and from this we get the term dinosaur, which means ‘terrible lizard’.

# Megalosaur

The falcon is one of our fastest flyers, and hunts for insects, lizards and even other birds. It can live for up to 10 years.

# New Zealand Falcon

# Ichthyosaur

This noisy seagull likes to look for food in all sorts of unusual places as well as along the coast – in parks and rubbish dumps, and around car parks, factories and shopping malls. It can live for nearly 30 years.

# Red-Billed Gull

**The starling is one of New Zealand's most common birds. It digs into soil with its bill to look for grubs and worms. It also eats spiders and snails, and can even catch insects while flying.**

## Starling

**This is probably the most famous of all New Zealand's shellfish. Though the paua shell shown here is well known for its bright colourings, the animal that lives inside is usually all black. Paua graze on seaweeds below the low-tide mark and can grow up to 16 centimetres in length.**

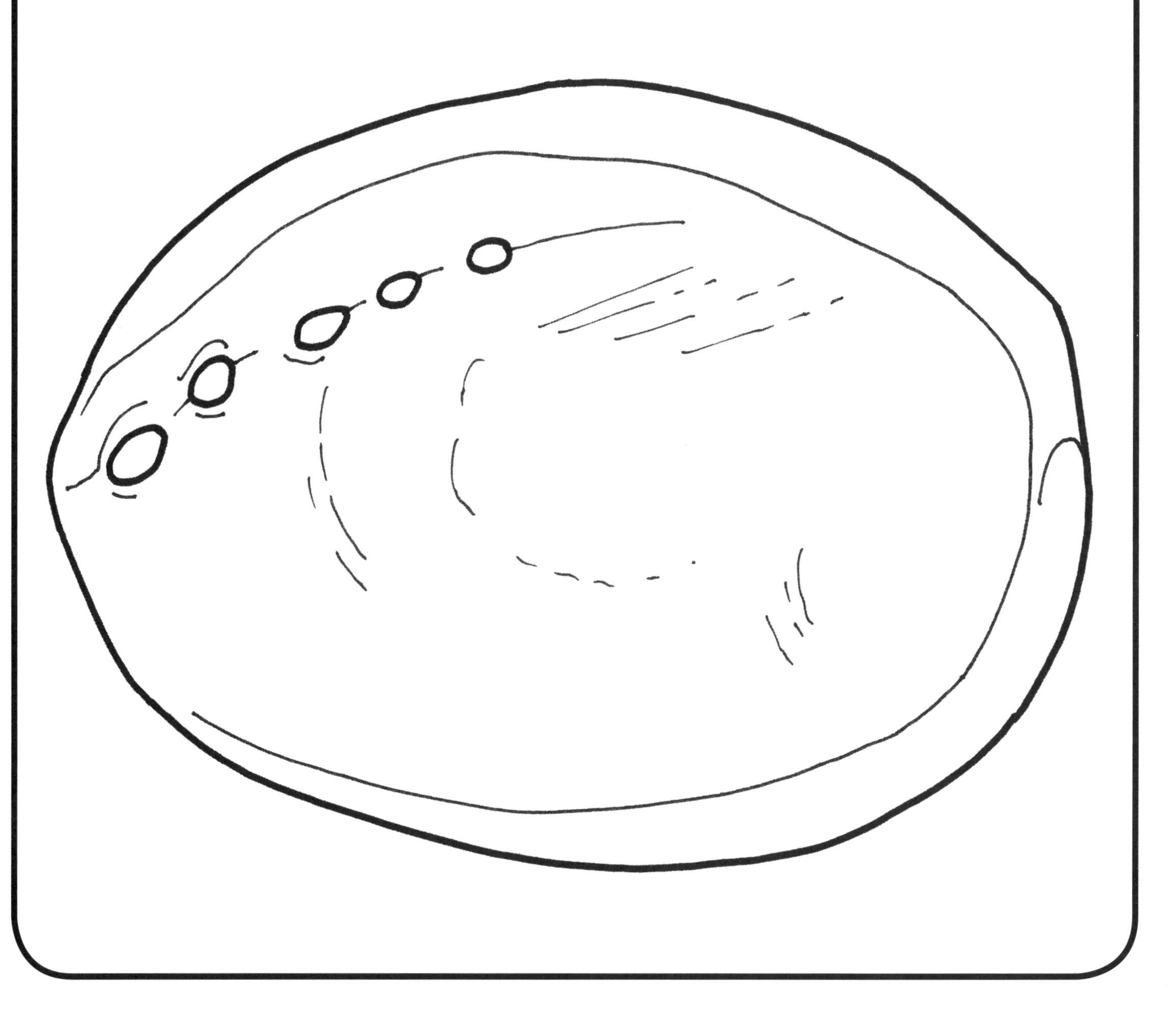

# Paua

**Once common around most of New Zealand, this frog became extinct around 1000 years ago. It was our largest native frog, with a body length of about 10 centimetres.**

# Waitomo Frog

**Like many other cuckoos, the shining cuckoo lays its egg in the nest of another bird, which then raises the cuckoo chick as though it were its own. The shining cuckoo spends the warmer months in New Zealand, but flies to islands around Papua New Guinea and Indonesia in the winter.**

# Shining Cuckoo

Like most other owls, the morepork hunts for its food at night. It has soft feathers at the edges of its wings that help it to fly without making any sound.

## Morepork

**Sea snakes have special adaptations for sea living. Their tails are usually flattened so that they can be used as strong paddles for swimming. Their long lungs allow them to stay underwater for 2–3 hours at a time.**

# Yellow-bellied Sea Snake

The pliosaur was the most fearsome hunter in ancient seas. Its skull alone measured 3 metres long and it was nearly 13 metres in total length. It fed on large fish and squid, turtles, sharks, ichthyosaurs and even on elasmosaurs.

# Pliosaur

**The weka cannot fly, but it is very good at walking and running! Nosy by nature, it happily enters campers' huts to look for anything edible, and will even steal any bright and interesting objects, such as watches, cutlery or compasses.**

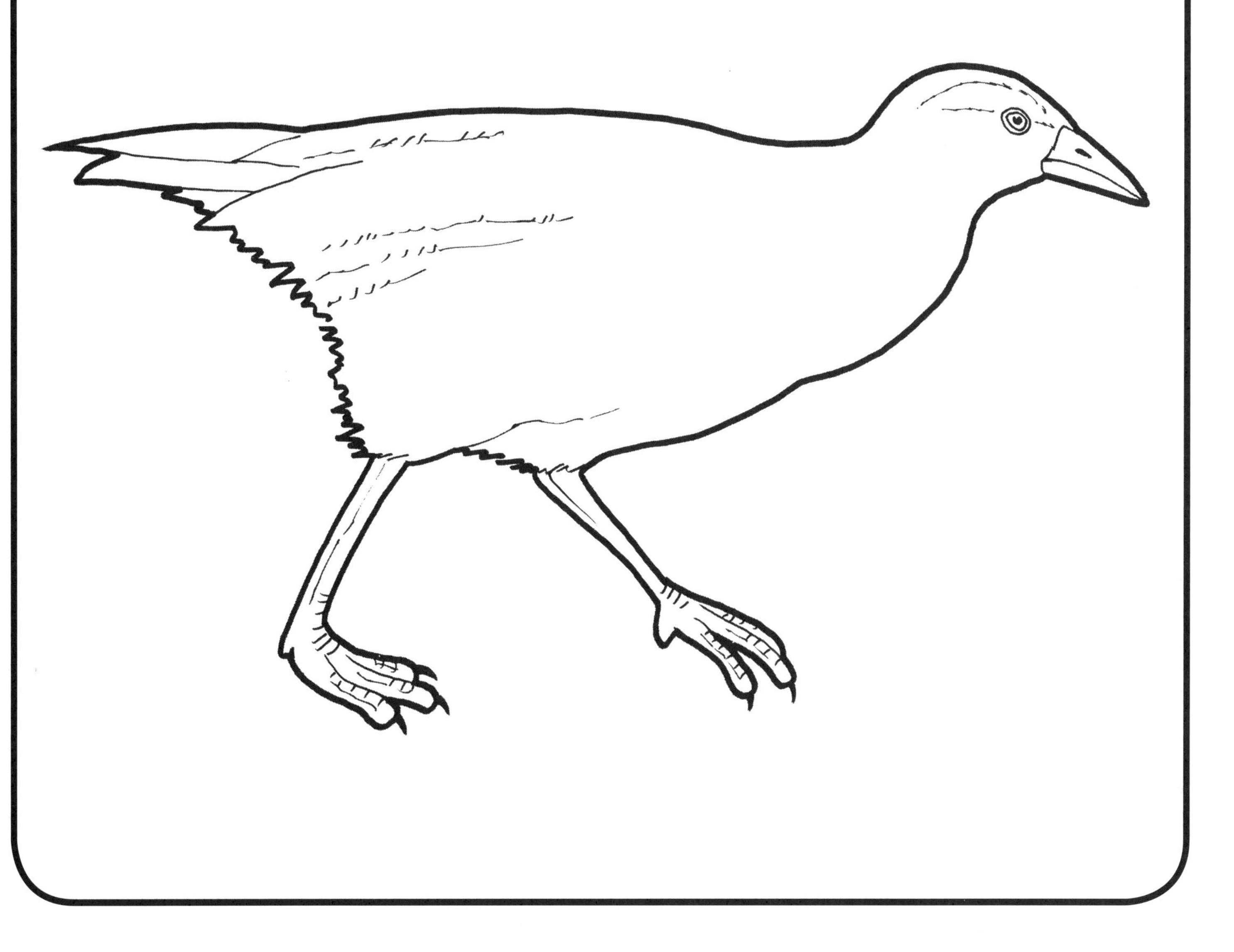

# Weka

The mudflat top shell is one of many species of small shellfish that can be seen in abundance around the mudflats of harbours and estuaries, and especially in stands of mangroves. It feeds on plant material. The top shell measures about 3 centimetres wide.

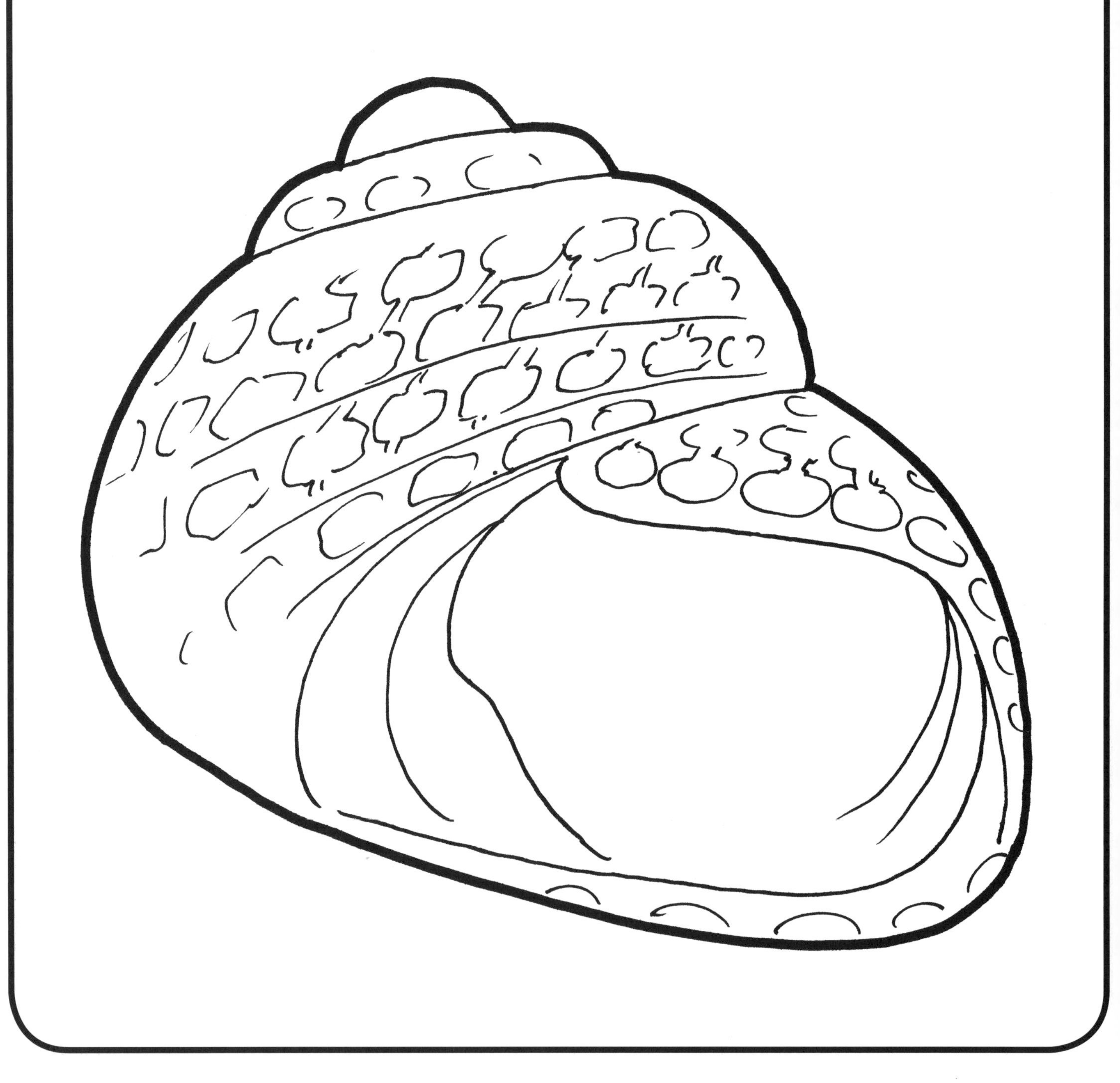

# Mudflat Top Shell

You'll often see this bird gliding and flying in lazy circles as it watches the ground for prey, such as rabbits, rats, lizards and small birds. It's often seen in the middle of a country road, too, hacking at the body of a dead possum or other animal.

# Australasian Harrier

**The very distinctive common rock crab is one of the best known of all the crabs on the shore. It can measure more than 4 centimetres across its back. It is common around wet rocks and pools in the mid-tide and high-tide zones, and can be quite aggressive if disturbed.**

# Common Rock Crab

The nautilus uses its many tentacles to snatch up small fish and crustaceans. The tentacles then pass the food to the nautilus's mouth, which, like octopus and squid, has a parrot-like beak. If it feels threatened, the nautilus closes down its large 'hood' and expels water out of its main siphon, to take off backwards like an underwater jetboat.

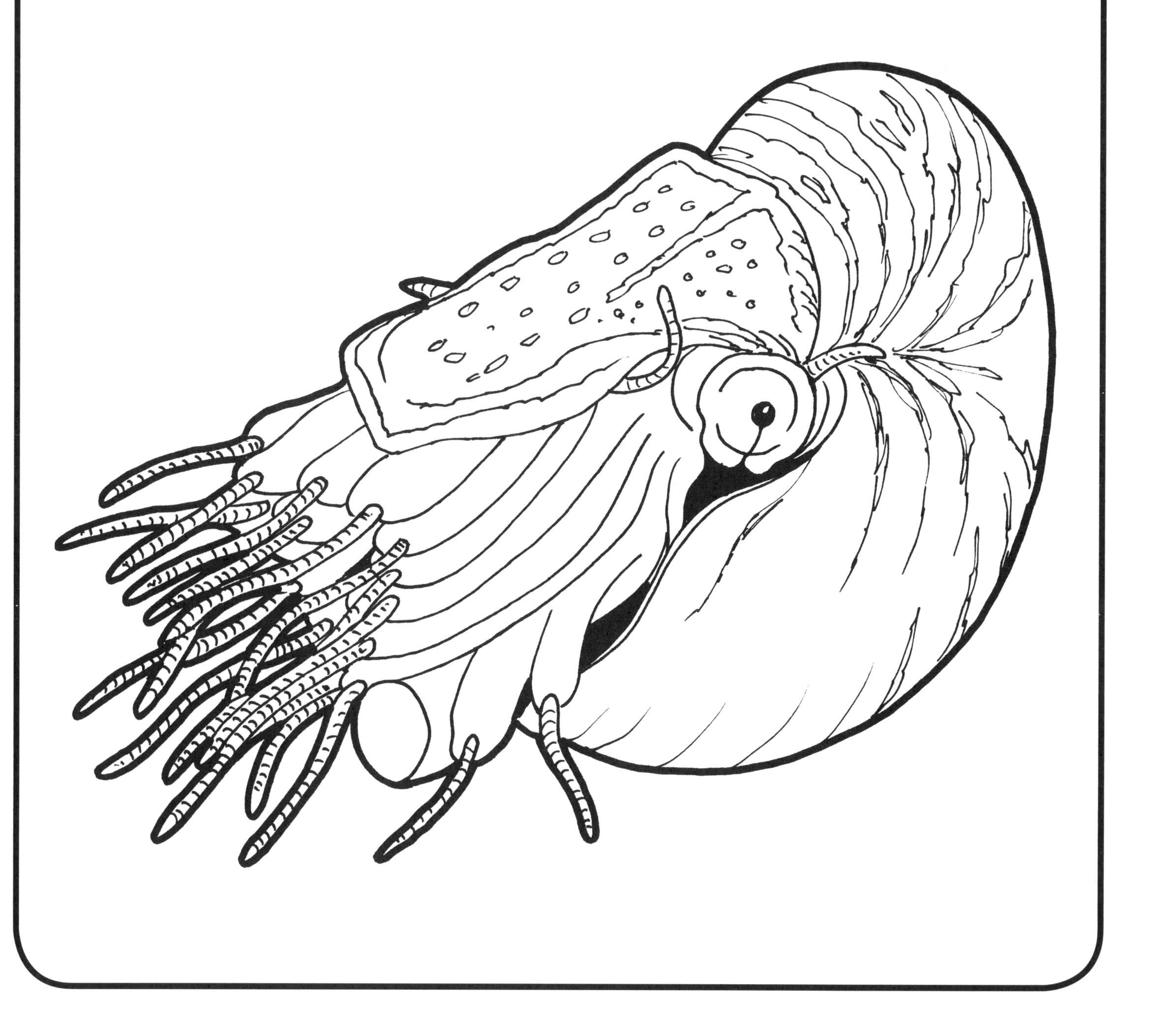

# Nautilus

The pukeko mainly lives in groups in wetlands and swamps. When it eats shoots or leaves, it holds its food in one foot – just like a parrot.

# Pukeko

Ankylosaurs were covered in thick bony plates and spikes. This armour helped to protect these slower-moving vegetarians if attacked by a megalosaur or allosaur. The New Zealand ankylosaur was about the size of a small car.

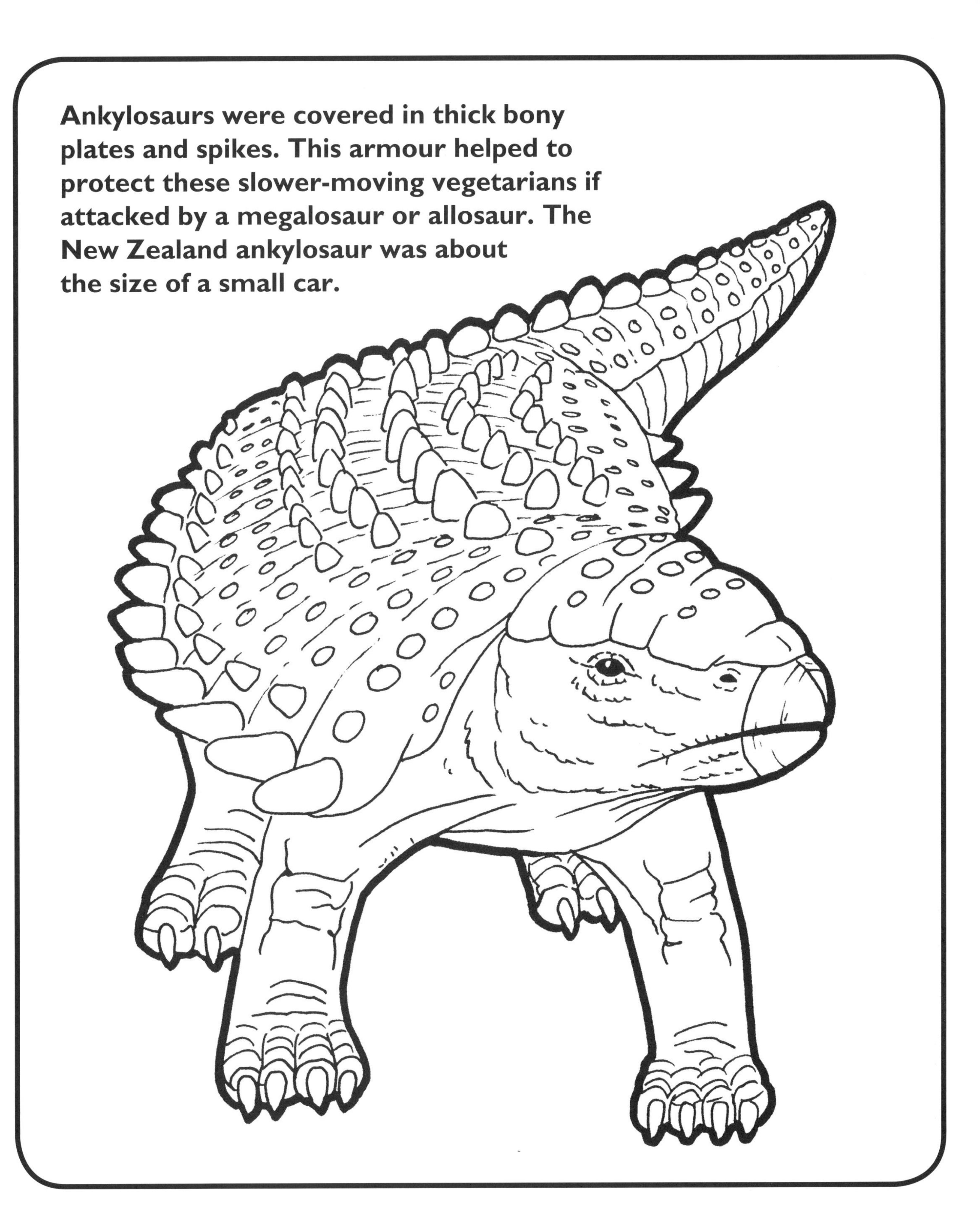

# Ankylosaur

**This large flightless bird had a strong bill that curved downwards like a woodworker's adze. This bill no doubt helped it to dig out prey from rotting logs or underground. The adzebill stood around 80 centimetres tall, and weighed 16 to 19 kilograms.**

# Adzebill

The bellbird has a very pretty song, which sounds like silvery bells. It lives in forests and eats insects and fruits, and can scramble and swing like an acrobat to take the nectar from hard-to-reach flowers.

# Bellbird

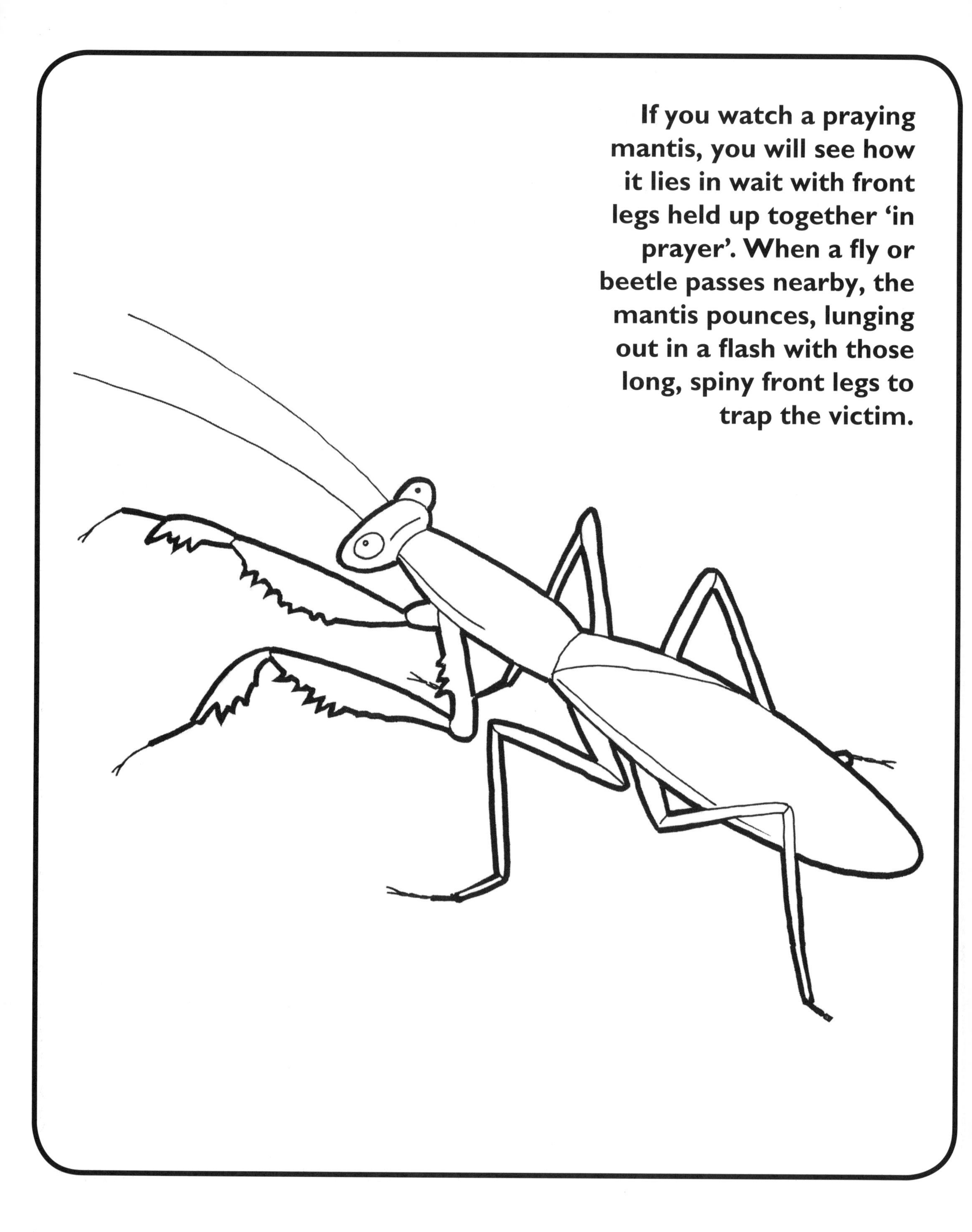

If you watch a praying mantis, you will see how it lies in wait with front legs held up together 'in prayer'. When a fly or beetle passes nearby, the mantis pounces, lunging out in a flash with those long, spiny front legs to trap the victim.

# Praying Mantis

The monarch is perhaps New Zealand's best-known butterfly, but it has only lived here for a century or so. Eggs are laid usually on swan plants; not much is left of the foliage by the time the striped caterpillars have eaten their fill.

# Monarch Butterfly

These coastal shorebirds can be seen in small groups or in flocks of hundreds – sometimes thousands. They use their strong bills to dig into the sand for worms, insects and even shellfish, which they open with a stab and twist of the bill.

# Pied Oystercatcher

# Extinct Land Mammal

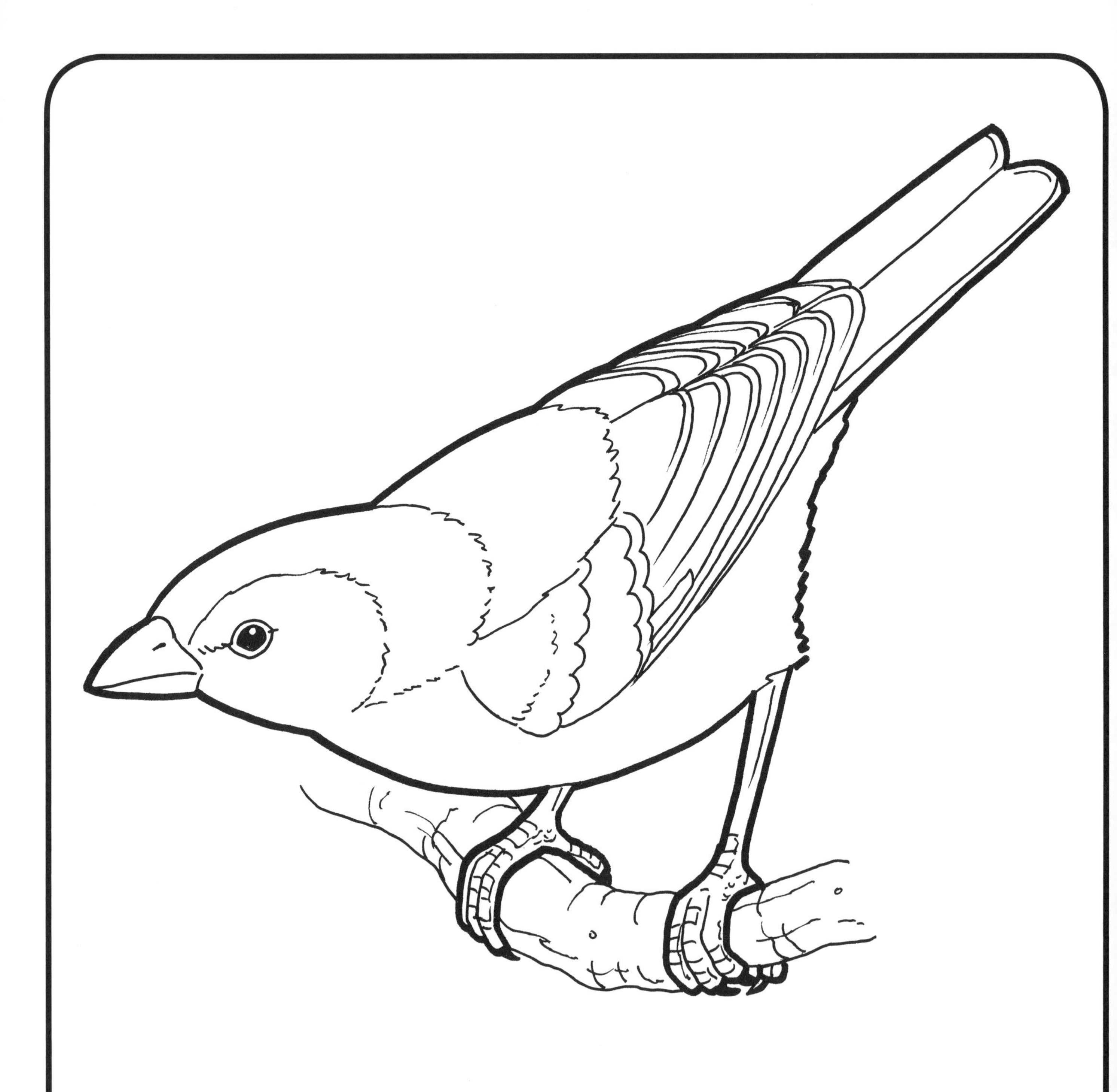

**The chaffinch was brought to New Zealand in the 1860s and has now spread throughout the country – some birds have even made it all the way to islands near Antarctica.**

# Chaffinch

The great white shark is a regular visitor to our seas. It is one of the deadliest hunters in the oceans around the world. It can dive to depths of 500–700 metres in search of prey, and sometimes can go as deep as 1200 metres. Great white sharks can reach up to 7 metres in length and can live for over 30 years.

# Great White Shark

The friendly little fantail often follows people as they walk through the bush, in order to catch any insects that might be disturbed. Fantails sometimes come into gardens and houses to look for other insects and spiders.

# Fantail

**This fearsome dinosaur was the largest meat-eater to have lived in New Zealand. It was related to the famous *Tyrannosaurus*, and was about 9 to 12 metres long. It ate other dinosaurs such as the hypsilophodont, ankylosaur and sauropod.**

# Allosaur

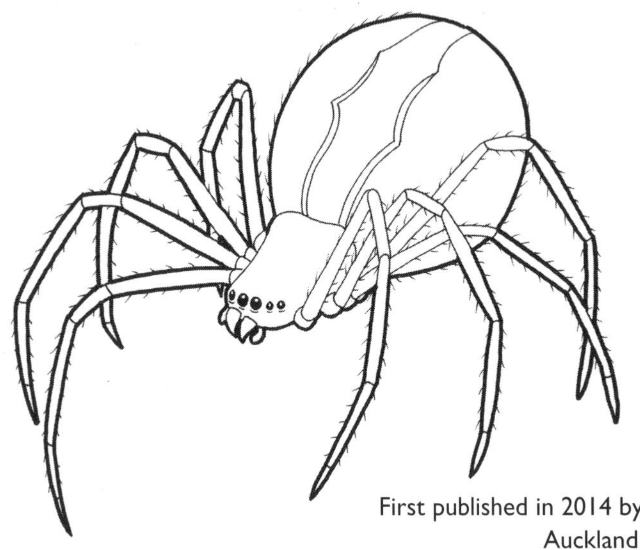

First published in 2014 by New Holland Publishers (NZ) Ltd
Auckland • Sydney • London
www.newhollandpublishers.co.nz

218 Lake Road, Northcote, Auckland 0627, New Zealand
Unit 1, 66 Gibbes Street, Chatswood, NSW 2067, Australia
The Chandlery, Unit 009, 50 Westminster Bridge Road, London,
SE1 7QY, United Kingdom

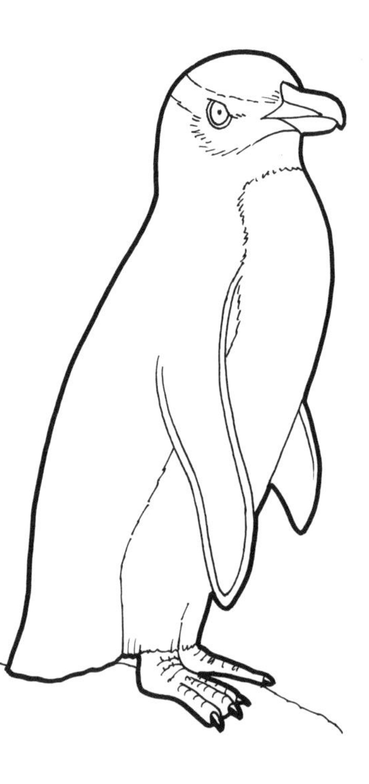



Publishing manager: Christine Thomson
Designer: Thomas Casey

ANational Library of New Zealand Cataloguing-in-Publication Data

Gunson, Dave.
The bumper book of New Zealand wildlife to read, colour and keep
/ Dave Gunson.
ISBN 978-1-86966-427-5
1. Animals—New Zealand—Juvenile literature. I. Title.
591.993—dc 23

1 3 5 7 9 10 8 6 4 2

Printed in Malaysia, by Times International Printers.